DOUGH SHALL NOT MURDER

AN IVY CREEK COZY MYSTERY

RUTH BAKER

CLEANTALES PUBLISHING

Copyright © CleanTales Publishing

First published in October 2022

All characters and events in this publication, other than those clearly in the public domain, are fictitious and any resemblance to real persons, living or dead, is purely coincidental.

Copyright © CleanTales Publishing

The moral right of the author has been asserted.

All rights reserved. This book or any portion thereof may not be reproduced or used in any manner whatsoever without the express written permission of the publisher except for the use of brief quotations in a book review.

For questions and comments about this book, please contact
info@cleantales.com

ISBN: 9798357254368
Imprint: Independently Published

OTHER BOOKS IN THE IVY CREEK SERIES

Which Pie Goes with Murder?
Twinkle, Twinkle, Deadly Sprinkles
Eat Once, Die Twice
Silent Night, Unholy Bites
Waffles and Scuffles
Cookie Dough and Bruised Egos
A Sticky Toffee Catastrophe
Dough Shall Not Murder
Deadly Bites on Winter Nights

AN IVY CREEK COZY MYSTERY

BOOK EIGHT

1

"Fall is my favorite season," sighed Betsy, blissfully sipping her pumpkin latte. "Don't get me wrong – summer's great! But something about the leaves changing color, and the night air becoming crisp…"

Lucy grinned at her young employee, who had decided to taste-test the bakery's new seasonal coffee flavor. "And pumpkin everything! The pumpkin chocolate-chip muffins are our top seller. They're selling out as quickly as Hannah bakes them."

Hannah came through the kitchen door at that moment, bearing a tray of pastries. "These guys might be a contender, though." She set the tray down for Lucy's inspection. "Caramel apple tartlets."

"They're almost too pretty to eat," Aunt Tricia commented. She chose one, holding it up to admire the fancy fluted crust. "But not quite." She bit into the pastry, murmuring her approval. Swallowing, she complimented Hannah. "Oh, my, those are divine!"

Hannah beamed and finished filling the glass pastry case. Turning to Lucy, she asked, "What's next, boss?" Her eyes twinkled. She and Lucy were old high school chums. When Lucy had taken over Sweet Delights Bakery upon the untimely passing of her parents, Hannah had stepped in to become the assistant baker.

Lucy glanced at the clock. "We still have fifteen minutes before opening. Let's go ahead and put up some Halloween decorations." She retrieved a box from under the front counter and brought it over to a table. The ladies crowded around as she opened it.

Betsy's eyes lit up. She reached in to pull out a string of mini lights shaped like pumpkins. "How adorable! These will look perfect in the front window!"

Aunt Tricia spied the electric Jack-o'-lantern and lifted that out next. "I think this will be just the thing for upstairs on the veranda." She headed in that direction as Lucy unpacked a few more decorations. A small, poseable skeleton... two gauzy ghosts about ten inches tall, equipped with loops to hang them...

Hannah laughed and held up a rubber bat suspended on a clear line. She flipped a switch on its back and the bat's eyes glowed red. "This guy is pretty spooky!"

Lucy chuckled and peered at the remaining items in the box. An assortment of colorful, synthetic fall leaves, and a scarecrow which would need to be snapped together. "I think these leaves will look great scattered in the front window, with the ghosts above them. The scarecrow can stand outside at the entrance, and we'll hang the skeleton on the inside of the door."

They each proceeded with their tasks, chatting conversationally.

"I met Joseph's younger brother, Derek, last night," Betsy announced, tacking up one end of the light string. "Such a nice guy! He's a sophomore at Hawthorn College, a theater major." Betsy was dating Joseph Hiller, who was the Ivy Creek Theater's production manager.

"Theater must be in the Hiller's blood," remarked Lucy. "Will Derek be in the November production of The Sword and the Stone?" She was looking forward to going to that play. The story of King Arthur had always been one of her favorite tales.

Betsy nodded, looping the string into a swag, and securing the midpoint. "He's trying for the lead. He would make a great young King Arthur." She looked over at Lucy, grinning, "I think he'll stop by soon and you'll get to meet him. I mentioned pumpkin muffins to him, and he practically drooled."

"We'll have to save him one," Hannah called out to Betsy with a smile. She finished hanging up the bat and ghosts and got down from the chair she'd dragged over. "What do you guys think?"

Lucy nodded approvingly, as Betsy finished stringing her lights and came to stand beside her. "Looks great, guys." She eyed the front window where she'd scattered the leaves. "Hannah, I think you and I should make an edible spooky house for the window display, too. The kids will love that."

Hannah grinned. "Sounds like fun!"

Aunt Tricia walked into the room, returning from upstairs. She looked at what they'd accomplished, and a smile curved her lips. "Well, ladies, I think we're ready for Halloween!" Glancing at the clock, she added, "And for business, too." She unlocked the door and flipped the sign to "Open", while Lucy positioned the scarecrow and skeleton.

Betsy returned to her station behind the front counter, organizing the flavored syrups next to the coffee machines, and Aunt Tricia opened the cash register, stocking it with bills. Hannah and Lucy stood in front of the pastry case, discussing their baking plans for the day.

"How many of those new caramel apple tartlets did you make?" Lucy asked.

"There's an extra dozen in the back," Hannah replied, then glanced at Lucy with a sly grin. "Are you thinking of bringing some to Taylor?"

Lucy felt her cheeks flush as she nodded. Taylor was the deputy sheriff in Ivy Creek and Lucy had recently begun dating him... again. They had once been high school sweethearts, but that had been a decade ago, and a lot of water had passed under the bridge since then. To say their relationship was complicated was an understatement.

The bell rang as someone entered the bakery, and Lucy turned to see who it was.

A young woman came forward, shyly saying hello. She carried a sheaf of papers and held one out to Lucy.

"Would you consider hanging this advertisement in your bakery?" she asked. "It's going to be a really fun Halloween attraction, and Mr. Marconi is hiring college students, like me, to play the monsters."

Lucy glanced down at the brightly colored flyer. *The Haunted Forest - A Hayride Full of Frights.*

"We sure will," she assured the young woman with a smile. "What a neat idea!" The girl thanked her, a pleased expression on her face as she left the bakery.

Betsy and Hannah crowded behind Lucy, reading over her shoulder.

Take a mile-long trip through the Haunted Forest, into the dark woods teeming with terror. You'll spot ghosts, goblins, and things that go bump in the night, guaranteed to make you shiver and scream. A Halloween adventure on a horse-drawn hay wagon, running Thursdays through Sundays in October. Come if you dare!

"Oh, how cool!" Hannah exclaimed. She looked at the address. "That's the old Sampson place. They have acres of woods out there."

Betsy commented, "That looks like a lot of fun! Joseph and I were talking about going to that haunted house attraction on the east side of town. What's it called?" Her brow furrowed.

"The House of Horrors?" Lucy asked. She'd heard the cashier talking about it at Bing's Grocery and wondered if it would be worth the admission price.

"Right!" Betsy snapped her fingers. "House of Horrors. But this actually looks more enjoyable, outside… under the moon…"

Hannah looked at the two of them, her eyes widening. "Hey, let's all go together! Kick off the spooky season with a bang. Or a Boo!" she joked. She looked over at Aunt Tricia. "What do you think, Tricia?"

Aunt Tricia smiled but shook her head. "I'll leave that sort of stuff to the younger crowd. But you girls should go."

Betsy ventured, "I bet Joseph and Taylor would go, don't you think?" She looked at Lucy.

Lucy smiled, amused by the notion of them all together on a spooky hayride. "I'm sure they would." She had a sudden thought and turned to Betsy. "Hey, didn't that girl say they were hiring college students to play the monsters? Maybe you should mention it to Joseph's brother, Derek."

Betsy nodded. "I was thinking the same thing. I'm sure he could use a few extra bucks. And it's acting… technically."

Hannah's face was filled with eager anticipation as she looked at her friends. "So, what do you guys think? Maybe Friday night?"

Lucy and Betsy exchanged glances and grinned.

"OK!"

"I'm in!"

"Excellent," Hannah proclaimed. She grabbed her apron off the hook, tying it around her waist. "This is going to be a blast!" She disappeared into the back to begin baking.

Lucy took the flyer to the front wall, tacking it up on the corkboard. She studied the colorful advertisement, smiling at the mental image of the five of them, *"kicking off the Halloween season with a Boo"*.

A night out in the crisp autumn air, under the moon, clinging to each other and squealing in mock horror. *A silly adventure*, she thought. *Lighthearted fun.*

She couldn't have been further off the mark.

2

The next morning, Lucy had just finished refilling the toffee candy display when a young man entered the bakery. She looked up, noting his dark hair and green eyes. Something about him seemed very familiar. As the fellow approached the counter, he flashed a smile, and she immediately knew who he was.

"You must be Derek Hiller," she deduced, her lips curving. "You look just like your brother." She extended her hand. "I'm Lucy Hale. Welcome to Sweet Delights."

Derek nodded and laughed, shaking her hand. "People say that all the time. I hope it's a good thing," he joked. He looked around with open admiration. "Wow, what a great place! I'd be as big as a house if I worked here."

Betsy's voice could be heard as she rounded the corner, a rag and bottle of Windex in her hand. "Good morning, Derek! I saw you cross the street from up on the veranda. Wait till you see the space upstairs. The view is awesome."

Betsy tucked her cleaning supplies away and crossed to the sink to wash her hands. Over her shoulder, she grinned at Derek and informed him, "You couldn't have had better timing. There are pumpkin muffins coming out of the oven any minute now."

Just as the words left her mouth, Hannah swung through the kitchen door, opening it with her hip. She carried a tray of steaming, jumbo-sized pumpkin muffins, studded with dark chocolate chips.

"Is someone wanting a muffin?" she asked as she pivoted. Her eyes landed on Derek and widened. "You must be Joseph's brother!" she exclaimed. "Wow, there's a really strong family resemblance."

Betsy chuckled and introduced Hannah. "This is Hannah Curry, our baker. And I wanted you to meet Lucy's Aunt Tricia, too, but she's off today."

"Well, I'm sure I'll be back," Derek assured her. His eyes lingered on the muffins, and he reached for his wallet.

Lucy beat him to the punch, wrapping a muffin in a napkin and handing it over the counter. "On the house," she said. "I remember college days. Money was always tight. And besides, Joseph is like family."

Derek thanked her, touched by her words. He looked to Betsy next, saying, "Speaking of money, thanks for the tip about The Haunted Forest, Betsy. I went over there last evening, and Mr. Marconi hired me on the spot."

Betsy clapped her hands, delighted, and Lucy and Hannah added their congratulations. Derek looked pleased.

"Monster or victim?" asked Hannah with a devilish grin.

"Monster," Derek grinned back. "Turns out luck was with me. Mr. Marconi said he'd already filled all the positions, and he'd been turning away other applicants. But he'd had to fire an employee just an hour before I came in. Their misfortune was my good luck, I guess."

"Why did he let someone go?" asked Lucy, curious.

Derek's expression sobered as he said, "Apparently, this guy, Russ something, came in drunk. And Mr. Marconi said it wasn't the first time."

Hannah nodded. "I think you're talking about Russ Leighton." She looked at Lucy. "I bet Taylor knows him. He gets locked up for being drunk and disorderly a lot."

"Oh," Lucy said, pitying the man. Alcoholism was a serious addiction.

Betsy changed the subject. "Grab your muffin, Derek, and follow me. I want you to see the veranda view."

Derek brightened. "Sure." He looked at Hannah and Lucy. "Nice to meet you."

"You, too," the ladies chimed together. Lucy called out as he walked away, "Hey, we'll be seeing you at work on Friday! We're all going to the Haunted Forest."

"Cool!" Derek grinned. "I'll be sure to be at my most scary!" He made a monster face and Lucy laughed as he walked away.

"He seems really nice," Hannah remarked, and Lucy nodded, thinking Friday night would be even more fun, now that they knew one of the actors.

Hannah returned to the kitchen, saying she had turnovers coming out of the oven, and Lucy stayed out front, manning the counter until Betsy returned.

She wiped down the blackboard they used for advertising specials and picked up the chalk, thinking about what to offer today.

Her back was turned when the door chimed again, announcing a customer. Lucy turned to see a man in his late thirties, with wire-rimmed glasses and thinning hair, wearing slacks and a button-down shirt. He looked around the bakery, taking it in.

"Welcome to Sweet Delights," Lucy said, cordially. "May I help you?"

The man met her gaze. His eyes were dark espresso in color, and strangely intense. His skin was pale, as though he didn't spend much time outdoors.

"Yes, hello," he said, his face very serious. "May I speak to Lucy Hale?"

Lucy approached him with a polite smile. "I'm Lucy."

He held out a hand and Lucy shook it. His skin was soft and uncalloused, and his palm felt slightly damp.

"Pleased to meet you," the man said. "My name is Bob Billings." His eyes searched hers hopefully.

Lucy didn't recognize the name. "Hello, Mr. Billings," she replied. "What can I do for you?"

His lips thinned, apparently dismayed that his name didn't strike a chord. "I'm a reporter," he informed her. "I used to have my own column with The Norton Sentinel. But I'm a freelancer, at present." Before Lucy could think of something to say to that, he hurried on.

"I'd like to do a story about you, and Sweet Delights Bakery."

Lucy smiled with genuine pleasure. *That would be great publicity, especially right now, as they were nearing the holiday season.* She nodded approvingly. "I would love to be interviewed. When would you–"

"Now." Mr. Billings interrupted her. "I would like to interview you now. If you have a few minutes to spare."

Lucy was nonplussed for a moment. Just then, Betsy and Derek came back downstairs, and Betsy resumed her station behind the counter. Derek waved goodbye, seeing Lucy was busy with Mr. Billings.

Why not? Lucy thought. She indicated a table by the window. "Sure. I have about fifteen minutes," she said. "Will that be long enough?"

Mr. Billings nodded, and they sat down. "I can always follow up on the telephone, if I have to." He pulled out a mini recorder and looked at Lucy for permission. With her nod, he hit a button and settled back, steepling his fingers.

"Lucy Hale, Sweet Delights Bakery," he intoned, then looked up. "First, Lucy, please tell me a little about how you came to own Sweet Delights," he requested.

Lucy gathered her thoughts for a moment, and began to speak, talking about growing up with her mother and father running the bakery. After only a minute or two, Mr. Billings interrupted.

"At the beginning of the summer, one of your employees was the prime suspect in the Fairy Tale Fair murder. Did you ever fear for your own safety?"

Lucy frowned. "My employee—who is also a dear friend of mine—was questioned and cleared early on."

Mr. Billings raised his eyebrows and changed tack. "You, Lucy Hale, were the one to find the murder weapon and a bloody princess costume in the bakery's dumpster. Tell us what went through your mind when you first laid eyes on the horrific evidence."

Lucy reached out and switched off the recorder, disgusted with the tabloid angle Mr. Billings was pursuing.

She stood up. "I'm sorry, Mr. Billings. I have no desire to contribute to an article that sensationalizes the tragedy that occurred in Ivy Creek last summer."

The man frowned as he tucked away his recorder, standing up as well.

"Ms. Hale, you're making a big mistake. Sweet Delights Bakery would get a lot of publicity from my story. A lot of folks would come from miles away just to see where the—"

Lucy shook her head firmly. "That's not the kind of publicity we want here."

She turned and walked away with a final, dismissive look over her shoulder.

"Good day, Mr. Billings."

3

Aunt Tricia shook her head, seated at the kitchen table with Lucy. Lucy had just returned home after her workday, to the house she and her aunt shared. It once had belonged to her parents, and Lucy felt comforted by the memories of growing up within these walls.

"That sort of article gives journalism a bad name," Aunt Tricia commented, denouncing Bob Billings and his intended story.

"I just hope no one else in town decides to talk to him," Lucy answered, absently stroking Gigi's tail as she rubbed against Lucy's leg. Gigi was Lucy's white Persian cat, and the feline ruled the household.

"I would think everyone in Ivy Creek would want to put that horrible incident behind us," remarked Aunt Tricia. She sipped at her tea, then looked at Lucy inquiringly. "Didn't you tell me you have a date with Taylor tonight?"

Lucy nodded, and a small smile crept onto her face. "He's taking me to dinner at Lorenzo's."

Aunt Tricia made an appreciative sound. "They have the best manicotti! But dear, maybe skip the garlic bread. You don't want to ruin a goodnight kiss."

Lucy burst out laughing. "Aunt Tricia! It's not like it would be our first kiss. And besides," she reasoned, "if both parties eat garlic, it cancels each other out."

Aunt Tricia smiled at her fondly. "I'm so glad you and Taylor have decided to give it another try. You two really were a great couple."

Lucy nodded, her thoughts drifting to her high school days. She and Taylor had been inseparable until Lucy decided to attend college in the city after graduation. As teens, they had never had a serious talk about the future, but Taylor loved small town life, and was quite content to stay in Ivy Creek. Lucy was dazzled by life in the city, choosing to stay and become a professional food blogger. They drifted apart, their romance fizzling out.

When Lucy had first returned to Ivy Creek after her parents' tragic death, Taylor had been quite cool to her, obviously holding a grudge. But gradually, as Lucy decided to stay and run her parents' bakery, he had warmed to her, becoming a solid friend she could count on. A spark of attraction had been rekindled, and a month ago, they had decided to begin dating again.

Aunt Tricia spoke, breaking Lucy out of her reverie. "Well, while you're enjoying your dinner at Lorenzo's, I'll be researching which book would be best to kick off my new book club."

"Oh, have you gotten everyone on board, then?" Lucy asked. Aunt Tricia had been trying for the last several weeks to convince a group of friends to start a book club, since they were all avid readers who often passed good books along to each other. Lucy thought it would be a great activity for Aunt Tricia, who would need a wintertime hobby to replace her gardening.

Aunt Tricia beamed. "Yes, there will be six of us, and we've decided to meet on Wednesday evenings, beginning next week. I'm thinking maybe we should start with a classic horror story first, since it's October, but I'm not sure which." She glanced at the clock. "What time is Taylor picking you up?"

Lucy looked at her watch and jumped up. "In an hour. I've got to go get ready."

THE EVENING WAS COOL, and as Lucy and Taylor strolled down Lincoln Street, she was glad she'd worn a sweater. They'd parked the car a block from the restaurant, reasoning they would want to walk off their dinner. The meal had been delicious. Lucy had ordered the lasagna, and Taylor, linguini with clams, and they had both eaten their share of garlic bread.

The experience of dining by candlelight had put Lucy in a cozy, romantic mood, and she looked up at Taylor's profile, giving his hand a squeeze. He smiled down at her.

"Warm enough?" he asked.

Lucy nodded and was about to speak when a commotion erupted on the sidewalk a few yards away.

"Don't tell me you're not trying to ruin my business! Just this week, you've caused three of my employees to jump ship!" A burly man in a leather bomber jacket hurled the accusation at another fellow, who stood defensively, hands on his hips.

"If you paid your employees a decent wage, they wouldn't come looking for a job at the Haunted Forest," the man retorted. He was smaller in stature but didn't seem cowed by the other man's anger. He glared up at the burly fellow, fire in his eyes.

His comment incensed the bigger man, who advanced, his hands fisted. "You're just afraid my House of Horrors is going to put you out of business! You're nothing but a hack with a hay wagon!"

Taylor stepped forward before the argument escalated further. He pulled aside his light jacket, flashing his badge.

"Easy, now, fellas. I'll have to ask you both to calm down." Taylor's tone was authoritative, and both men took a step backward, though the bigger fellow still glared menacingly at the other man.

"You better keep to your side of town, Marconi," the man spat out, his face twisted with anger. "Stay away from my hires, if you know what's good for you."

With that, the big man turned and stalked away, leaving Taylor eyeing him disapprovingly.

The other man flashed an apologetic smile. "I'm sorry, ma'am," he nodded at Lucy before meeting Taylor's gaze. "And officer. My apologies you had to witness that."

Lucy nodded, accepting his sentiment. "You're Carl Marconi, who runs the Haunted Forest attraction?"

Mr. Marconi nodded, his expression still troubled. "Yes. Apparently, Willie Childers doesn't think Ivy Creek is big enough for both our Halloween attractions. His House of Horrors was the only game in town last year." He shrugged dismissively.

Taylor assured him, "Oh, I think we have enough citizens looking for some Halloween fun that both attractions will get their share of customers."

Lucy added, "Our friend Derek Hiller was just hired by you. We're all planning to come to the Haunted Forest on Friday night."

Mr. Marconi grinned, his mood lightened. "I'm so pleased to hear that! Well, I hope you have a great time. Enjoy your evening."

They parted ways, and Lucy and Taylor resumed their walk. As they reached the car, Lucy's mind circled back to Willie Childers, and his raging animosity toward Carl Marconi. It left a sour taste in her mouth.

She was glad she and her friends had chosen the Haunted Forest to patronize, over the House of Horrors. Spooks and monsters aside, she found Mr. Childers' temper to be pretty scary.

4

The next day, Lucy and Hannah were caught up enough on their baking to begin making an edible spooky house for the front window display.

"So, is this like a gingerbread house?" asked Betsy, watching Lucy carefully cut out cardboard templates for the walls and roof.

Lucy nodded, her eyes on her razor knife. "Exactly. Only it's made out of chocolate sugar cookie dough instead of gingerbread."

Hannah was busy rolling out the dough, and Lucy passed her a finished template for the gable walls.

"The trick is," Hannah continued tutoring Betsy as she cut the dough around the template, "You need to trim the house pieces square when they're partially baked, but then pop them back in the oven until they're good and hard, and almost singed on the edges."

Betsy watched in rapt attention. "Why is that?"

Lucy had finished cutting her templates and was now unwrapping butterscotch candies and placing them in a food processor. "Because humidity is your enemy when it comes to building edible houses. You have to overbake the walls, and especially the roof, so that once it's assembled it won't sag over time."

Hannah finished cutting the house pieces and popped the tray in the oven. "The cool thing is, we're going to make this a light-up house, using crushed butterscotch candy for the windows."

"Neato!" Betsy smiled. "The kids walking by are going to love that!"

Lucy grinned, picturing the neighborhood kids gathered in front of the bakery window on a crisp October evening.

She finished crushing the candy and then moved on to preparing the base board for under the house. She cut out a large rectangle from a thick piece of foam core board, marking off the dimensions for the house, and then cut out a small access panel from the center.

She looked up at Betsy. "So, we'll build the house on this board, and once it's all assembled and the icing is dry, we can use a small battery powered light inside, placing it through the cut-out panel from underneath."

Hannah piped up. "This year, Lucy found a light that flickers, as well as making spooky noises, so it'll be really cool!"

The scent of the chocolate dough baking wafted over them, and Betsy sniffed the air appreciatively. "That smells delicious!"

She watched as Hannah slid a tray out of the oven and laid templates over the partially baked pieces, trimming them square with a sharp knife. Next, Hannah sprinkled some crushed butterscotch candy in the window holes. Task completed, she set the tray back in the oven to melt the candy and bake the pieces longer.

"So, what holds the walls and roof together?" Betsy asked, finding the process very interesting. She thought maybe next year she could make an edible spooky house as a surprise for Joseph.

"Royal icing," answered Lucy and Hannah simultaneously. They looked at each other and laughed. Lucy added, "It's the cement of the baking world. The same stuff you put gingerbread houses together with."

Aunt Tricia poked her head around the corner. "I smell chocolate cookies. Any samples?"

Hannah indicated the trimmings from the walls, and Aunt Tricia's eyes lit up. "Oh, yes, with a glass of milk, perfect for a pick-me-up." The door chimed out front and Lucy peered around the corner.

"It's Joseph," she announced, and a smile lit up Betsy's face. She was at the counter in a jiffy, telling Joseph all about Lucy and Hannah's project.

Lucy and Aunt Tricia joined them a moment later, just as Betsy finished rattling off what she'd learned.

Joseph smiled back absently at Betsy, but his eyes gave away his mood, lacking their usual twinkle.

"What is it?" Betsy asked, her brow wrinkled. He seemed sad.

Joseph sighed. "You know Derek had his heart set on playing the lead in The Sword and the Stone…"

They all nodded, and he continued. "Well, for obvious reasons, I stepped down from casting this one, and hired Tim Ferreira as the casting director. He just posted his choices this morning."

He looked at Betsy's worried face. "Derek didn't get the part. Tony Newton will be playing the young King Arthur."

"Oh, no," Betsy said, dismayed. She knew Derek had wanted that role more than anything. He'd spent hours rehearsing for the audition.

Lucy and Aunt Tricia murmured sympathetic responses, and Joseph nodded glumly.

"Worse still," he said, "Tony and Derek have a long history of rivalry, all through high school. Since they were both interested in theater, naturally they would always be pitted against each other for roles. And then, in senior year, they both pursued the same girl… and things got ugly."

"Oh, no. Did they fight?" asked Lucy. She remembered some hotheads in high school vying for the attention of the same young women. Things could get out of hand quickly.

Joseph nodded. "I'm afraid so. In a restaurant over in Colby, and the police had to be called." He hastened to add, "No one was hurt, and since they were both minors, their parents just had to come pick them up. But… it deepened the animosity between them."

His green eyes clouded. "I was afraid something like this would happen as soon as I saw both of their names on the sign-up sheet. I know I'm biased, but Tony Newton isn't the most gracious winner. He's seen this as a personal victory. He's taunting Derek about it on social media, calling him a talentless loser."

"Uh-oh..." Aunt Tricia said. "Have you talked to Derek, tried to get him to focus on something else?"

Joseph nodded. "He just said I didn't understand and stormed out. I'm hoping he doesn't do something stupid, like seek Tony out and start trouble. Derek's young, and he's hot-headed, and right now, he's not seeing the big picture. He's too old to get in a brawl. Unlike last time, he's not a minor. There would be consequences."

Lucy tried to console him. "Maybe his new job at the Haunted Forest will serve as a good distraction. And we'll all be there in a few days, and we can pump him up. I'm sure he'll have a good time dressing up and playing a monster."

Joseph shook his head ruefully. "Unfortunately, Derek's job might add fuel to the fire." He looked at the three women, who wore identical puzzled expressions.

"Tony Newton works at the Haunted Forest, too."

5

Lucy had just turned on the ovens and was about to make herself a cappuccino when she heard Hannah unlock the back door. She waited, a greeting on her lips, but suddenly, she heard Hannah talking to someone. Her voice was low and soothing, the cadence of which you'd use when speaking to a child.

Intrigued, Lucy stepped over to the partially opened door and peered out.

Hannah was crouched in the back parking lot, her hand outstretched. The early morning light was dim enough that at first Lucy couldn't see who her friend was speaking to. Silently standing in the doorway for several seconds, she waited, and finally saw movement by the dumpster.

"It's OK," Hannah cooed. "You can come out. I won't hurt you."

The sleek black head of a cat peeked around the corner of the metal container, its green eyes wary. It studied Hannah carefully, taking a hesitant step forward. The cat was not quite full grown, Lucy noted, and seemed very skinny.

"Aw, you poor baby…" Hannah kept her hand outstretched, and her voice low. "You've had a rough time of it, haven't you?"

The cat blinked and rubbed the side of its face against the metal corner, not coming closer, but yearning for attention. Hannah clucked her tongue and made kissing noises, but the kitty stayed where it was, just watching.

Finally, Hannah straightened up, sighing. The cat bolted at the sudden movement, and Hannah turned to come inside. She jumped when she saw Lucy at the door, and chuckled, a hand at her throat.

"Oh! You startled me!" She followed Lucy into the warm kitchen. "Did you see that black cat?"

Lucy nodded. "Poor thing. Looks like a stray."

Hannah took off her jacket, her eyes troubled. "Skinny, too. Probably hungry." She reached for her apron with a contemplative expression. "Don't we have a few cans of tuna in the stockroom?"

The bakery often ran lunch specials of homemade soup and sandwiches. Lucy grinned at her friend's soft heart. "I believe we do…"

Hannah laughed at Lucy's expression. "I know, I know. I'm a sucker for animals. But winter will be here before you know it. It's already pretty chilly at night. I hate to think of that poor baby suffering."

Lucy cocked her head. "Does your apartment allow for pets?"

Hannah shrugged. "It doesn't say anything in the lease, but my landlord is reasonable. Probably, with a pet deposit, I could have a cat." She tapped the counter thoughtfully.

"I'm getting ahead of myself. I need to make friends with the kitty first." She disappeared through the doorway, heading for the stockroom. "I owe you a can of tuna, Lucy!"

Lucy smiled. It would be good for Hannah to have a cat. Hannah had always been close to her sister, Pam, but Pam had recently moved away. Although she knew Hannah had some friends in town, every night after work, the young woman went home to an empty apartment. Lucy knew from her own experience with Gigi: a cat to cuddle with after a long day was a comfort, indeed.

Hannah returned moments later with a small paper plate loaded down with chopped tuna. She passed through the kitchen, heading for the back door, and Lucy couldn't resist following her to watch.

After Hannah set the plate a safe distance away from the building, she backed up, joining Lucy in the doorway.

Only a few moments passed before the sleek, black feline reappeared, looking warily at the women, and sniffing the air. With its bright green eyes watching them for any sudden moves, the cat approached the dish and gobbled down the food. The tuna was gone in less than a minute. After licking the plate clean, the kitty sat placidly and washed its face, before standing and giving the girls one last measuring look. With a swish of its tail, it disappeared behind the dumpster.

Lucy and Hannah both sighed and returned to the kitchen.

"I think I'll ask around," decided Hannah. "It looks like a stray, but I'd better make sure."

Lucy smiled. "Do you think you can make friends with her? Or him?"

Hannah nodded confidently. "I bet I can. And I have a gut feeling that it's a girl."

The ladies discussed their workday plans, listing pastries that were low in stock on the whiteboard on the wall, which served as their to do list.

"Are you going into town for supplies?" asked Hannah, flipping open their enormous recipe book and leafing through it.

Lucy nodded as she fixed the metal paddle in place on their Hobart mixer. "Probably at midday. If you can think of anything we need, just tell me, or add it to the list."

Hannah glanced at Lucy with a grin. "Kibble," she ventured. "Tricia will skin me if I use all the tuna."

Lucy chuckled, making a mental note. "That she would," she agreed.

She really hoped Hannah was able to make friends with their feline visitor.

———

IN THE PARKING lot of Bing's Groceries, Lucy was loading her purchases into her car when she noticed something peculiar happening across the street. There was a man moving along the cobblestone walkway in front of the shops, pausing at each of the posts that held up the awnings. He carried a tote bag, and his large frame looked familiar. From where she stood, she couldn't tell who he was or what he was doing.

He was either putting something up or taking something down. *Or... both?*

Her curiosity piqued, she finished loading her car and shut the hatch, locking it. She crossed the street and shaded her eyes, looking after the man's retreating form. When he turned slightly, she saw his profile, and it clicked into place why he looked familiar. It was Willie Childers, she realized.

But what was he doing?

From her current vantage point, she saw now she had been right. Mr. Childers was systematically taking flyers down from each post, and stuffing them into a plastic grocery bag, before reaching into his tote bag and tacking a new flyer up.

Curious, Lucy kept an eye on him as she walked up to the nearest post. It wasn't much of a surprise when she saw what the man was hanging up.

It was a new advertisement for the House of Horrors, the orange and black flyer proclaiming it to be "The Best Halloween Fun in Ivy Creek", and also promising a "Newly Added Graveyard!"

Well, there's no harm in that. Advertising the House of Horrors more widely makes good business sense.

Still, she was curious why he'd been taking down flyers. Were they the old flyers, perhaps, before the new graveyard addition? Mr. Childers was still within her line of sight, and Lucy regarded him, head cocked.

He had apparently finished with his task, and she saw him cross to a wire trash bin and toss his plastic bag in, before continuing down the street. Chiding herself for being too nosy for her own good, Lucy walked over to the receptacle and peered inside. She reached in and withdrew a wadded-up ball of paper, uncrumpling it, and smoothing it out. What she saw had her lips thinning with annoyance, her sense of fair play offended.

It was a flyer for the Haunted Forest. Mr. Childers was removing all the flyers Mr. Marconi had posted and replacing them with his own.

Lucy frowned in the direction Mr. Childers had gone, deciding she would tell Derek to give his employer a heads up. As she crossed the street again to reach her vehicle, she shook her head in disgust.

Some people would do anything to win.

6

"Well, I guess we'll be in line for a bit. Does anyone want a hot cider? I see a vendor over there." Taylor nodded in the direction of a stand a few yards away.

Lucy nodded, zipping up her jacket, and Betsy and Hannah chimed in their own affirmative response.

"Great idea," Joseph said, offering, "I'll go with you."

The men headed in the direction of the vendor, and Hannah retrieved her gloves from her jacket pocket, slipping them on. It was a chilly night, but the sky was clear, and the moon was beginning to rise through the trees.

Betsy's eyes sparkled, her cheeks rosy from the nip in the air. "I'm so glad we came! This is going to be a blast." Filled with anticipation, she focused on the forest ahead of them, from which muted screams and peals of laughter could be heard.

Speakers set up high on wooden posts piped classic Halloween music, adding to the atmosphere. The strains of "Monster Mash" by Bobby Pickett drifted over the crowd.

Lucy looked at the long line forming behind them. "Apparently, Mr. Childers' unsportsmanlike behavior didn't affect ticket sales."

She'd shared what she'd witnessed in town with the others, and Betsy had told Derek, who had alerted Mr. Marconi that his flyers were down.

"I think word is spreading that it's a great attraction," Hannah said. "Sometimes word-of-mouth is all you need."

The line moved up a few feet. Lucy calculated that their turn would come in about ten minutes. She watched as a family of five clambered up onto a wagon loaded with hay bales to sit on, the mother instructing the children to hang on to the rails. With a cluck of his tongue, the driver set the horse to a steady walk, heading into the shadows of the spooky woods.

"Derek says he'll be dressed in a werewolf costume about halfway into the ride," Betsy informed them. "He's going to pop out from behind an old cabin."

"How long does the ride last?" asked Hannah.

"Twenty minutes or so," Lucy volunteered absently, "I read it online." She had suddenly noticed a familiar figure off to one side, some distance away. *Was that Bob Billings?*

The man in question turned, and Lucy saw the camera looped around his neck. She was right. The reporter took a few pictures of the crowd waiting in line, and some more of the jack-o'-lanterns and scarecrow that were placed at the entrance. Lucy watched him, her eyes narrowed. She was still irritated with the man's eager questioning regarding last summer's tragic murder in Ivy Creek.

"What is it?" Taylor asked her, returning to the line.

He handed Lucy a cardboard cup crowned with a cloud of fragrant, cinnamon-spiced steam. Lucy accepted the beverage gratefully, taking a tiny sip. Hot apple cider was perfect for this weather, and it did the trick, warming her up nicely.

"Oh, it's nothing," she assured Taylor. "Thank you, this is great."

Out of the corner of her eye, she saw Mr. Billings proceed down the Haunted Forest trail on foot. *He must be doing a story on the attraction.*

Suddenly, there was a commotion ahead of them, and Lucy heard a man's voice raised in argument.

"I'm here to do what I was hired for! Now, get outta my way!" The words were slightly slurred, and the tone belligerent. Lucy stood on her tiptoes, looking over the heads of the crowd.

She saw a man with long, stringy hair who looked to be about thirty, weaving and wobbling on his feet. He shook his finger at the employee manning the gate.

"You don't tell me! Marconi is my boss, not you!" He attempted to brush past the hapless employee, but then stumbled, managing to regain his footing with arms flailing.

"That's Russ Leighton," Hannah whispered to Lucy. "The guy that got fired."

Joseph looked at Hannah in surprise. "I didn't know Russ worked here. He does janitorial work at the theater. I've always felt kind of sorry for him."

Taylor frowned and glanced at his friends, saying, "Be right back."

He strode forward, just as the frustrated employee pulled out his cell phone to place a call. The young man acknowledged Taylor with a grateful nod, turning away to speak into his phone.

"What's going on here, Russ?" Taylor asked, keeping his tone pleasant.

Russ turned to regard Taylor, not recognizing him in street clothes.

"I work here," he informed Taylor haughtily. "What's it to you?" He narrowed his eyes with hostility.

"He *used* to work here, but he was fired," corrected the employee in a low tone, swiveling back around. He tucked away his phone. "Mr. Marconi is on his way."

Taylor nodded, turning to advise Russ. "I think you should head on home now, Russ. You don't want me to have to bring you in, make you sleep it off in a cell tonight."

Russ blanched, suddenly recognizing Taylor. "I didn't do nuthin' wrong, Officer. I work in there." He pointed to the trail, swaying slightly on his feet. "As a zombie," he clarified.

Mr. Marconi suddenly appeared, walking up from the parking lot. "Mr. Leighton. You *do not* work here anymore. I've already hired your replacement." He glanced at Taylor. "Thank you, Officer."

Taylor nodded and refocused his gaze on Russ. "Did you hear that, Russ? You were let go. This is not your job anymore."

Russ blinked and frowned at Mr. Marconi. "Fired me? Well, of all the..." He turned to regard the forest trail wistfully, seeming uncertain of what to do next.

Taylor looked over at his friends. The line had moved up, and their turn was coming up soon. Lucy hoped Taylor wasn't going to have to miss out on their ride.

Taylor eyed Russ impatiently, issuing a stern warning. "Go home, Russ. If I come back out and see you here, I'll be bringing you in to the station."

The man nodded morosely; his gaze still fixed on the forest trail. He turned around slowly, mumbling to himself, and began to wander away, casting a few backward glances to see if Taylor was still watching him.

"Do you think he'll really leave?" Lucy whispered to Taylor. Russ had stopped at the edge of the parking lot and was staring at the thick woods, his hands twitching at his sides.

Taylor sighed. "I think he will, eventually. But if he's still on the grounds when our ride is over, I'll have to bring him in."

Lucy nodded. *It was sad, really.*

Just then, their wagon pulled up, and Lucy tried to shake off her sudden melancholy, stepping forward with her friends.

Joseph and Taylor assisted the girls up onto the wagon, and they all settled comfortably against the hay bales. Lucy exchanged excited smiles with Betsy and Hannah. She squeezed Taylor's hand as the driver clucked to his horse.

With a lurch, the wagon moved forward, away from the light and sounds of the parking lot. The looming trees closed in around them, and moonlight filtered through the branches in sharp splinters.

Lucy's spine tingled with anticipation as she eyed the shadowy trail winding through the forest. She was ready for some old-fashioned, frightful fun.

7

The wagon bumped and rocked, meandering down the hard-packed trail. The bushes were hung with tiny orange, twinkling lights, and fake spider webs decorated the trees. Up ahead, Lucy could see the first staged scene, illuminated by an electric lantern hung on a tree.

The wagon approached, slowing its pace as they drew up beside it, and Lucy and her friends watched the scene play out.

Two gravediggers worked with shovels and picks, laboring next to an open grave. Crooked headstones sprouted from the earth around them, and the lantern light flickered eerily over the actors' faces, made up to look gaunt and ghoulish. As the gang watched, an arm shot out of the open grave, dragging one of the workers down into it, while he screamed and struggled. The other gravedigger turned to flee, and a monstrous figure stepped out from behind a tree with a cackling laugh, dragging the hapless gravedigger away through the forest, as he flailed his arms and called for help.

Despite herself, Lucy's arms erupted in goosebumps, and she glanced at her friends, wide-eyed, as the horse plodded on.

"OK, that was pretty startling," confessed Joseph with a laugh.

Betsy had covered her face with her hands and now peeked out nervously between her fingers. "Is it over? I couldn't look once the guy got pulled into the grave."

Hannah hooted with laughter, while Taylor smirked. "C'mon, Betsy! If you close your eyes, you'll miss all the fun!"

Just then, a hooded figure rushed at the slow-moving wagon, dressed in a red cape, with skeleton make-up glowing on its face. "Bwaa-haa-haa!" The creature gripped the railing of the wagon, trotting beside them and startling Hannah, causing her to shrink away.

"Doom and destruction lay ahead," the figure intoned in a scary voice. The wagon driver clucked his tongue, and the horse increased its pace, leaving the ghoul behind.

"OK, that was intense," confessed Hannah, shaking her head with a rueful laugh. "Well done."

Lucy smiled at her friend and glanced up at Taylor. He put his arm around her shoulder, hugging her close. "I'll protect you," he whispered teasingly, and a warm, fuzzy feeling came over her, adding to her enjoyment of the night.

They passed several more scenes, all laid out very well, with the wagon slowing at each one so they could appreciate the actors. A crazed clown rushed the wagon, brandishing a hangman's noose and "looking for a volunteer". A group of gauzy-costumed ghosts flitted through the trees, peeking out from behind the trunks and stage-whispering, "Here it comes… it's looking for you…"

Betsy hid her face against Joseph's chest as they passed a vampire scene next. Bloody victims lay deathly still beneath a flickering red light, and dozens of bats were suspended on wires from tree branches. A black-caped figure stood in the center of the clearing, white face paint standing out starkly, with rivulets of blood painting his mouth. The creature raised his arms as if about to take flight, and hissed at them, displaying his fangs.

"They must go through gallons of fake blood here," commented Taylor, as they rumbled on.

"Kind of a messy job for the actors, too," added Hannah.

The wagon approached a slight hill, and at the top, Lucy could see a structure. It looked to be an abandoned cabin.

"Hey, isn't this Derek's station?" she asked Joseph.

He nodded, and Betsy straightened up, peering ahead. The group waited in high anticipation as the rustic shelter came into view. Obviously built long ago, the wooden boards were rotted, with the roof caved in and the door hanging crookedly, half open. The windows were devoid of glass, and vines crawled through the structure, adding to its eeriness.

The wagon slowed, and the group collectively held their breath, waiting for a werewolf to emerge. Seconds passed, but Derek never showed. The wagon continued to roll slowly forward, and soon the structure was behind them.

"What happened?" Betsy asked, craning her neck to look backward. "I thought that was Derek's post."

Joseph shook his head, frowning, obviously puzzled. "I don't know."

"Maybe they were short-staffed, and Derek got moved to another spot," ventured Lucy, trying not to be disappointed. She'd really been looking forward to seeing Derek play his part.

"Maybe," agreed Betsy, hopefully. "He was originally going to play the zombie role, but he said he got switched to the werewolf. Maybe they switched him back."

The group settled back in, preparing for the next scene. The horse plodded sedately on, rounding a bend where the trail narrowed.

Suddenly, the animal snorted fearfully and stepped sideways, tossing its head.

"Whoa, there," said the driver. "Steady now."

The animal whinnied and danced, snorting and high stepping, obviously spooked. The driver kept a tight rein, speaking in a soothing tone, but the horse wouldn't settle down, instead balking and trying to rear.

The wagon rocked, and the girls gripped the railings, looking at each other in alarm.

"I'll give you a hand," Joseph called to the driver, hopping down. "I grew up around horses."

Taylor addressed the girls. "Let's get out while they calm the horse, just in case."

He hopped out and assisted the ladies, one at a time, while Joseph held the bridle of the animal, talking it down, and petting its neck.

"What in the world was that all about?" Lucy wondered out loud, standing on the path. They were far enough into the forest she could no longer hear the hubbub of the parking lot.

Betsy glanced around at the woods apprehensively. "I have to say, the horse acting so scared isn't calming *my* nerves any…"

Hannah consoled her. "There's probably a fox nearby or something, is all. Horses can be very skittish at night."

"So can I," muttered Betsy, rubbing her arms and casting Joseph a longing look.

Taylor frowned, peering down the trail ahead of them.

"What is it?" Lucy asked him.

He shook his head. "Probably nothing." Despite his words, he began to walk down the path, and Lucy followed him, shivering with a sudden chill.

A few yards ahead, the path curved again. Rounding the bend, Lucy could see the next scene, set in a brushy area off to the right. A rusted out, abandoned Volkswagen Beetle was spray painted with the words, "Too Late", and a homemade sign proclaimed the "Zombie Apocalypse". Fake severed limbs were scattered about, grotesque under spotlights fixed to trees. A "bloody" sheet was hung to appear as a half-hazard tent, and a black cast-iron kettle rested ominously inside a fire ring filled with ashes.

"OK, this one is going to scare Betsy to death," Lucy joked, her voice sounding unnaturally loud to her own ears. Her words seemed to echo in the stillness. "I better give her a heads up."

Taylor didn't answer, staring fixedly not at the scene, but at a point ahead on the trail. He continued slowly forward, and

Lucy trailed behind him, her eyes suddenly widening in surprise.

Laying directly across the hard-packed trail was an actor, wearing a rubber zombie mask and shredded clothing.

"Hello!" Taylor called out, approaching the figure. Lucy clutched at his arm nervously.

The actor didn't move as they reached him. His eyes, visible behind the mask, were wide open and staring, and his neck and shoulders were covered in fake blood.

A sudden, coppery smell assaulted Lucy's senses, and she gasped, stepping back with a horrified realization.

That wasn't fake blood. This actor wasn't acting.

8

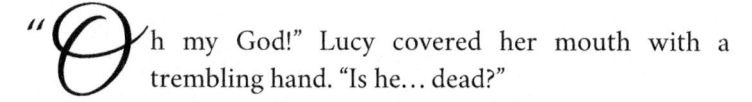

"Oh my God!" Lucy covered her mouth with a trembling hand. "Is he... dead?"

Taylor knelt swiftly at the man's side and reached for his wrist, checking for a pulse. Lucy could feel her own heart galloping in her chest. She scanned the dark forest, her scalp prickling uneasily.

Taylor looked grim as he straightened, pulling his police radio from his jacket.

"Stay right here," he instructed her, turning around to speak briefly into the device. With a static pop, he concluded his call, and turned back to Lucy, taking hold of her arms gently.

"Yes, the man is dead," he confirmed soberly, then added, "The police are on their way. I'm going to take you back to the wagon now and—"

Taylor stopped speaking, looking up sharply, as they heard a clattering coming down the trail. Apparently, Joseph had calmed the horse. The wagon was approaching the zombie set with a slow, steady, clop-clop. Joseph and Betsy waved at them enthusiastically, and Hannah called out a cheery "hello", unaware of the crisis.

"Stop right there!" Taylor boomed out, holding up a palm.

The driver immediately reined in the horse, looking confused.

"What's wrong?" called Joseph, hopping out of the wagon. Hannah and Betsy followed suit.

Lucy glanced down at the body with a horrified thought. "Taylor, what if it's Derek?" *Derek hadn't been at his assigned station. Had his role been switched back to zombie?*

Taylor looked at her, then at the body, and then at Joseph. The indecision was apparent on his face. Their friends were only twenty feet away now.

Joseph suddenly spied the body, and took the decision out of Taylor's hands, running the rest of the way at full speed. He skidded to a stop before them.

"Who is that?" he demanded; his face full of panic. "What happened?"

Taylor held up a hand to Hannah and Betsy, who had halted in shock some distance away. "Please, stay right there."

He grabbed Joseph's arm, stopping him as the man bent toward the body, a trembling hand reaching for the mask.

"Let me," Taylor said, locking eyes with Joseph. "I need to preserve the scene."

Joseph nodded, and Taylor gingerly took hold of the edge of the rubber mask, carefully pulling it up and away from the actor's face. Lucy held her breath, praying the man was not Derek.

The lightly bearded face revealed was unfamiliar to her, and she breathed a huge sigh of relief. Joseph looked over at Taylor with a quick shake of his head, then closed his eyes briefly, getting a hold of his emotions.

He opened his eyes again and peered down into the young man's face, eyes widening as recognition dawned. His expression was troubled when he looked back at Taylor.

"That's Tony Newton."

Lucy, Hannah, and Betsy stood together beneath the glare of the parking lot's lights, fidgeting, while Joseph paced back and forth, his cell phone tightly pressed to his ear. Derek's whereabouts were still unknown, and they were waiting for an update from Taylor.

Joseph returned his phone to his pocket, anxiety marring his handsome features.

"Anything?" Betsy asked, searching his face with worry.

"Nope." Joseph shook his head, lips compressed. "Went straight to voicemail. His phone must be shut off."

Derek's pickup truck was still in the lot, so they knew he was still at the Haunted Forest. *But where?*

Police had swarmed the scene shortly after Taylor had radioed in, and an officer had driven the four of them back to the parking lot in an all-terrain vehicle. Most of the crowd had been dispersed, with an officer positioned at the gate to take down everyone's name before they were allowed to leave.

As Lucy watched the shadowy entrance to the woods, she spotted another all-terrain vehicle emerging. It stopped at the edge of the pavement, and the driver and passenger both got out. The passenger looked odd, and after a second, Lucy realized why. The figure was wearing a furry costume, though his head was bare. He carried a shaggy mask in his hands.

"Look, it's Taylor and Derek!" Lucy announced to her friends with relief.

"Oh, thank goodness!" said Betsy, and Hannah exhaled a deep breath, clasping her hands.

"Thank God," said Joseph, emotion clogging his voice.

The men approached the group, and Lucy caught the worried expression on Derek's face. *Where had he been?*

Joseph voiced her thoughts, striding forward and embracing his brother.

"Where were you, Derek? Are you OK?" His forehead was creased as he looked from Taylor to Derek.

Derek's face was pale, his eyes round with shock. He was clearly shaken by the events. Taking a deep breath, he explained.

"When I arrived at the cabin, there was a note hung on the door, saying I needed to play my part at a different location - at the marsh area on Loop C. But when I got there, I saw a chain had been put across the trail."

Seeing their puzzled faces, he clarified, "A chain means that section of the trail is closed. The hayride isn't going to Loop C tonight."

Taylor reached into his jacket and pulled out a handkerchief, folded around a paper. He unwrapped it carefully and displayed the note for the others to see.

"Don't touch it," he warned.

They all peered together at the yellow paper. A sentence was written in unfamiliar handwriting, backing up Derek's words, and a crude map with an "X" showed Derek where he was needed. Taylor carefully wrapped up the note again, tucking it away.

"I don't understand," said Betsy, beetling her brows. "Why would someone send you to a closed part of the trail?"

Joseph looked at Taylor, frowning. "Maybe because the cabin was so close to the zombie set? The killer didn't want any witnesses?"

Taylor's face was impassive. "Maybe," was all he said. Lucy had a sinking feeling that the killer had another reason for sending Derek away, and she wondered if Taylor had the same suspicion.

Just then, an officer strode forward, calling out Taylor's name. The group huddled in silence as the officer approached. He held a large object encased in an evidence bag.

"We just found this in the woods, sir. Looks like the murder weapon," the man said. "It was hidden in the brush behind the old cabin." He held out the bag, and Taylor accepted the grisly package carefully.

It had taken two evidence bags to fully encase the long, skinny object, and the clear plastic had become smeared with blood, obscuring the details. Lucy's breath caught with a sudden realization: the contents of this bag may have ended a young man's life just hours before.

Taylor turned the bag over and held it up to the light, and the weapon was clearly defined. Derek blanched, rocking backward, his face turning even paler.

Joseph spoke up, his voice strained with urgency.

"Taylor."

The deputy looked at him sharply, and Joseph continued, his eyes wide with alarm.

"I recognize that… it's a prop from the theater. That's the sword from our new production."

The Sword and the Stone, Lucy thought, with an involuntary glance at Derek.

The play in which Derek had lost the lead role to Tony.

9

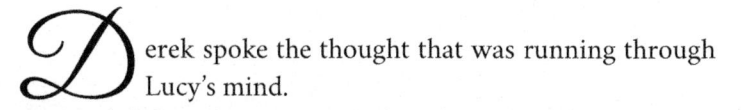

*D*erek spoke the thought that was running through Lucy's mind.

"Someone is trying to frame me!" His eyes were wild as he looked around the group. "Whoever killed Tony sent me away on a wild goose chase, so I wouldn't have an alibi!"

Taylor looked thoughtful. "We won't know anything until the coroner examines the body. We'll process the sword for prints and maybe we'll get lucky."

"But my fingerprints will be on that sword!" exclaimed Derek, clearly panicking. "You guys know I could never… Joseph," he turned to his brother, grabbing his arm. "You know I didn't do this!"

Joseph spoke calmly, though his eyes were troubled. "Of course, I know you didn't, Derek. Don't worry, we'll get to the bottom of this." He looked back at Taylor. "Could the note be of any use? It's not Derek's handwriting."

Taylor nodded solemnly. "We'll process that for prints, as well. But handwriting analysis is not what you see in the movies," he warned. He looked at the group, meeting everyone's eyes. "I need you all to keep quiet about the evidence – both the note and the murder weapon. If word gets out, it will make this case even harder to solve."

The group murmured their assent and grew quiet again. Everyone was clearly shellshocked by the events of the evening.

"Joseph, who had access to the props?" Taylor asked.

Joseph frowned. "Well, anyone who was trying out, I guess. The costume and prop room aren't kept locked."

"And if the theater was locked? Who had a key?"

Joseph closed his eyes, thinking. "Myself, the casting director, Tim Ferreira... oh, and Russ Leighton." His eyes popped open, realizing the significance.

Taylor nodded grimly, and Lucy wondered if they had just discovered the motive for the killing.

"The theater is just five minutes from here," Hannah added, her eyes wide. "Do you think–"

An authoritative voice suddenly rang out, interrupting her speculation.

"Derek Hiller!"

Lucy turned to see Mr. Marconi striding forward, his mouth set in a grim line.

"I've been told you were MIA tonight, even though you clocked in at your scheduled time. Where have you been? All three wagon drivers reported there was no werewolf at the cabin tonight." He looked angry, and Lucy saw Joseph stiffen, taking a protective step toward his brother.

Derek's tone was defensive. "I was–" He glanced at Taylor and stopped. *Was he allowed to mention the note?*

Taylor stepped forward, handling the situation. "Apparently, Mr. Hiller received a communication instructing him he was needed elsewhere on the grounds. We're investigating the situation, and I can't share any more details with you at this time."

Mr. Marconi's eyes narrowed. "A communication from whom?"

Taylor shook his head. "We're not releasing any more information just yet." He glanced at Derek's worried face. "I should add, though, that when Mr. Hiller realized he'd been misdirected, he tried to return to his regular post. One of the officers spotted him, en route there, and brought him to me."

Mr. Marconi was silent for a moment, his brows drawn together. It was obvious he had more questions. Finally, he fixed Derek with a hard look, saying, "Until this is all resolved, you're on probation, Mr. Hiller. Be aware I'll be keeping an eye on you."

He looked at Taylor next. "When will I be able to open back up? Not to be insensitive, of course."

Taylor pursed his lips. "It might be as long as a week. This is a big area to process. We'll have to be sure we don't miss anything."

"A week!" exclaimed Mr. Marconi. He shook his head and sighed. "The season will be at the tail end by then. I'm not sure it'll be worth keeping the power on if we can't run for a week."

He turned to regard Derek suspiciously. "A secret communication, huh?" The words were scornful as he turned on his heel and left.

Derek's shoulders slumped immediately. "Mr. Marconi doesn't believe me," he said, looking depressed.

Joseph put a hand on Derek's shoulder. "It will all work out," he said. "Trust me."

Just then a flashbulb went off, and Lucy blinked, seeing spots.

"Hey! You play the werewolf, right?" a familiar voice sounded, before peppering Derek with questions. "Several drivers claim you were missing tonight. Are you a suspect? Did you just get fired by your employer? Do you have any comment?"

Bob Billings had elbowed his way into their circle, and now Derek stood, blinking, trying to formulate a response. The flashbulb went off again, and Joseph stepped forward, angrily.

"You, there… get out of his face!"

Mr. Billings frowned, regarding Joseph inquisitively. "And you are?" He suddenly noticed the strong resemblance between Derek and Joseph and raised his eyebrows. "You two must be family. Do you have any comment about–"

Taylor cleared his throat for attention, and Mr. Billings glanced his way, eyes widening when Taylor flashed his badge.

The man recovered quickly, eagerly asking, "Are you questioning this employee? Is he a suspect?" He lifted his camera again, and Taylor held up a hand, saying sternly.

"Stop."

Mr. Billings lowered his camera reluctantly. "The people of Ivy Creek have a right to know what's going on, officer."

Taylor corrected him. "It's Deputy. Deputy Baker, Mr....?"

"Billings," the man replied, adjusting his glasses. "Bob Billings, freelance reporter."

"Mr. Billings, did you take pictures inside the Haunted Forest tonight?"

The man looked proud, unable to resist the opportunity to brag. "I most certainly did. I was granted exclusive behind-the-scenes access and took pictures of the sets before the customers arrived. This is going to be a blockbuster of a story, especially now that someone was..." he suddenly looked abashed. "I mean..."

"Yes, I know exactly what you mean," Taylor said, thinly veiled disgust coloring his tone. He held out his hand. "Your camera, please, Mr. Billings."

The man gaped at him, speechless for a moment. Taylor waggled his hand impatiently.

"But... but..." Mr. Billings sputtered, reluctantly unwinding the strap from his neck and passing the expensive Nikon over. "That's private property!" he blustered.

Taylor nodded. "Yes, and it will be returned to you. But, as you pointed out, you had behind-the-scenes access. You could very well have captured evidence tonight that will aid in our investigation. We'll have an expert look over the footage."

His hands full now, Taylor nodded to the group. "I've got to get back. You all go on home now. Derek, Joseph, I'll need your statements down at the station tomorrow."

Taylor walked away, with Bob Billings dogging his heels, pestering him.

"Aren't I supposed to sign a form or something? That's a very expensive piece of equipment…"

"Let's go," Joseph said, looking at the group. "It's been a long night. Derek, I want you to stay at my house tonight."

Derek nodded wearily, in no mood to be alone. He said goodnight to the ladies before heading to his pickup truck.

Betsy, Joseph, Hannah, and Lucy walked across the parking lot together, each lost in their own thoughts. There were very few cars left, the lot mostly full of police and emergency service vehicles.

Arriving at Joseph's car, Lucy noticed a flyer tucked under the wiper blade.

Joseph plucked it off, holding it down for the rest of them to read.

It was an advertisement for the House of Horrors, promising two-for-one admission.

As Joseph shook his head and crumpled the paper, Lucy realized there was one person who would benefit from tonight's tragedy.

Willie Childers now had the only Halloween attraction in town.

10

"I can't believe it," said Aunt Tricia, shaking her head. "How awful... and poor Derek!"

Her aunt had been asleep when Lucy got home, and when she'd woken this morning, Aunt Tricia had already left for the bakery. They were now sitting at a table on the bakery's veranda with Betsy and Hannah, filling her in on the events of last night.

Betsy added worriedly, "The problem is, all the evidence so far points to Derek. He can't prove he didn't write that note himself, and he and Tony were known rivals."

Lucy frowned. "Taylor isn't the sort to jump to conclusions." She was worried, though, that Joseph's brother would have a hard time clearing his name.

"Don't forget, Russ Leighton was there, too, behaving badly. Getting fired and replaced by Tony could be construed as motive. And also, he had the opportunity to steal the sword," Lucy pointed out.

Hannah nodded. "I think Russ will be questioned today... if they can find him." The man had been nowhere in sight when the group left the attraction last night.

Betsy suddenly peered over the railing, seeing a police cruiser pull into their lot. "That's Taylor, now."

Lucy got to her feet, hearing the ladies follow as she made her way downstairs. The bakery wasn't due to open for another fifteen minutes. She crossed to the front door, opening it just as Taylor was reaching for the knob.

"Good morning. Did you sleep?" she asked worriedly.

Taylor's face showed proof of the long night he'd put in. He shook his head and pulled Lucy close for a moment, dropping a kiss on her forehead. Stepping back, he met her eyes.

"Coffee?" he asked hopefully, and Lucy nodded, leading him to a table.

He looked around at the women gathered close by, questions plain on their faces. Everyone held their tongue, however, until Lucy returned with a steaming cup of black coffee, setting it in front of Taylor with an apple turnover.

"Thanks." He sipped the strong black brew and sighed, looking at the pastry. *News before food*, he decided.

"We dusted the sword for prints," he informed them. Lucy could tell from Taylor's expression that it had been in vain. He focused on Betsy. "The only prints we found were Tony Newton's, Joseph's, and Derek's."

Betsy slumped, defeated. "Maybe the killer wore gloves..."

"What about the note?" asked Hannah.

Taylor shook his head. "Just Derek's prints."

Lucy bit her lip, thinking. "Did anyone get a chance to look through Bob Billings' photos yet? Maybe there's something on there."

Taylor broke off half of the turnover, devouring it, and washing it down with coffee before answering her. "Someone will be evaluating the film today."

He looked troubled, glancing out the window. "We're still on the lookout for Russ Leighton. If any of you see him, I need you to call the station immediately."

He finished the rest of his turnover in one bite and stood up, downing the remaining coffee. "I've got to get back to the station. Derek and Joseph are supposed to come in at 9:30 to give their official statements."

Lucy kissed his cheek and walked Taylor to the door, watching as he crossed to his cruiser. With a heavy heart, she flipped the bakery's sign to "Open".

Despite the events of last night, she had a business to run.

THE MORNING WENT BY SWIFTLY, as Lucy and Hannah stocked up on fall treats, and Betsy and Aunt Tricia assisted a steady flow of customers. Around eleven o'clock, Lucy was evaluating the pastry case when the bell jangled, and Derek walked in. Lucy greeted him, noting the shadows under his eyes, then introduced him to Aunt Tricia.

"You poor boy," Aunt Tricia said, concern on her face. "I heard about what happened. I want you to know we're all standing behind you."

Derek nodded his thanks and attempted a smile, but it fell flat. Betsy came around the side of the pastry case and led him to a chair.

"Let me get you a coffee and a pumpkin muffin," she offered. "Are you just back from giving your statement?"

He nodded. "Yes. Joseph said to tell you he'd call you later. He had to get to the theater."

He seemed dispirited, and Lucy's heart went out to him. He was so young to have this sort of trouble ensnare him. She slid into a chair across from him as Betsy returned with the beverage and pastry, taking a seat herself.

"Thanks, Betsy," Derek said, his face brightening a bit. He broke open the chocolate-chip studded muffin and popped a piece in his mouth. "So good," he murmured appreciatively.

The women let him eat in silence for a moment, then Betsy asked hesitantly, "How did it go at the station?"

Derek grimaced. "Not exactly a fun time. Another officer kept asking me if I had access to the theater after hours, even though I told him no. He didn't seem to believe me."

"Where was Taylor?" Lucy asked, frowning.

"Interviewing Joseph," the young man replied. He sipped his coffee contemplatively. "He talked to me afterward." He glanced up, suddenly remembering he had news to share.

"They finally found Russ Leighton."

Betsy perked up; her eyes wide. "Really? Where?"

Derek shook his head. "I didn't recognize the name, but I think it was the parking lot of a bar. Asleep in his car."

"Did you hear anything else?" Lucy asked, hoping this meant the police had nabbed the killer. "How did Russ look?" *Did he have blood on him?* She didn't want to say the words, but if Russ was covered in Tony's blood...

Derek frowned. "I only saw him for a second. He looked a bit... unkempt, I guess."

Lucy was silent. Russ had looked pretty unkempt since the last time she'd seen him. She suspected that was his usual look.

"So, what happens now?" Betsy asked, nibbling her bottom lip anxiously.

Derek sighed, brushing the muffin crumbs into a napkin, and rising to his feet. "All Taylor told me was not to leave town. I guess we'll just have to wait and see what the police come up with."

He said his goodbyes and left. Betsy and Lucy returned to the counter, where Aunt Tricia consoled Betsy. "I'm sure Taylor will get to the bottom of this, dear. Don't fret."

Lucy agreed, walking back into the kitchen to join Hannah. After filling her friend in on what Derek had said, Hannah shivered. "Well, I hope they decide to keep Russ locked up for now. Out of anyone, I'd say he had the most motive, and he seemed half out of his head when we saw him. That's pretty scary."

Lucy countered, "What's pretty scary is the thought that a murderer might be loose in Ivy Creek if it turns out not to be Russ."

The women fell back into their usual rhythm of work, with Lucy whipping up a batch of royal icing to be used later on the spooky house, while Hannah added piped pumpkins and ghosts to a Halloween cupcake order.

A half an hour later, the phone rang, and Aunt Tricia appeared in the doorway, receiver in hand. "It's Taylor, Lucy," she said, passing her the handset.

"Hey, what's up?" greeted Lucy, walking away from the noisy, open oven. Hannah was unloading a batch of praline cheesecakes, and the sound of the fan made it hard to hear.

"Have you seen Derek?" Taylor asked without preamble. He sounded tense.

Lucy frowned. "Yes, he was here a little while ago. Why?"

Taylor didn't answer, instead asking, "Did he say where he was going? He's not with Joseph, and he's not answering his cell."

Lucy's heart raced. *What was happening?*

"No… he didn't mention his plans. What's going on, Taylor?" She gripped the receiver, knots forming in her stomach.

Taylor was silent for a moment. "I just had a visit from Tony Newton's parents."

Lucy waited, knowing it was never easy dealing with the family of a murder victim.

Taylor sounded grim. "The officer who questioned Derek says he asked him if he'd ever had a physical altercation with Tony before."

Lucy shut her eyes, knowing where this was going.

"Derek lied, Lucy. He told the officer he hadn't. But Tony's father told me Derek and Tony were taken into the Colby police station for brawling in public, two years ago."

Taylor continued crisply. "I just called the Colby police to check, and it's true. If they hadn't been minors, both boys would have had to appear in court, but they caught a break. The arresting officer decided to just call their parents and send them home with a stern warning."

Lucy didn't know what to say. Her mind raced. *Obviously, Derek had only lied because he was scared, but...*

Taylor put her thoughts into words.

"Lying to the police... it looks bad, Lucy. Like he's hiding something. If we can't locate Derek by the end of the day, I'll be forced to put out an APB on him."

11

That evening, Lucy was at home, sitting on the sofa with her cat Gigi, when the phone rang. Her mind was a million miles away, and the ringing didn't register for a moment.

"Lucy?" her aunt called from the kitchen. "Are you going to get that?"

Lucy hopped up, displacing Gigi, who flounced off, swishing her tail in annoyance. Lucy grabbed for the phone, almost knocking over a plant in her haste.

"Yes? Hello?"

It was Joseph. "Hi, Lucy. I just wanted to let you know Derek is OK." Joseph's voice sounded apologetic. "I know everyone was worried when he didn't answer his cell earlier, but apparently, he'd left it on the charger."

Lucy frowned. "Left it on the charger? But where was he?"

Joseph sighed. "He says he was just walking around town, trying to clear his head. You know, this whole situation is really freaking him out. And I know he's afraid the police think he's guilty."

Lucy felt bad for Derek, but she felt like she had to point out the error of his ways. "He lied to the police, Joseph. They asked him if he and Tony had ever gotten into a fight, and he said no. That, in itself, has made him appear guilty."

Joseph sounded glum. "I know. I explained that to him. He's down at the station now, talking to Taylor. He was just scared, Lucy. He said the officer who questioned him was very aggressive, insinuating that Derek had written that note himself, and not believing that he didn't have a key to the theater. I think he was afraid they'd lock him up if he told them about the brawl."

He hurried on, "I'm not excusing his behavior, Lucy. But… Derek's only twenty. He makes a lot of mistakes."

Lucy's expression softened, thinking of herself at twenty. It was true, that was a tender age, and people were bound to make mistakes as they grew up.

"You're right, Joseph," she said. "Twenty is a messy age. Thanks for letting me know. I'll talk to you soon."

They both hung up, with Lucy wondering how Derek's second interview with Taylor was going.

THE NEXT MORNING WAS BRIGHT, and it seemed like the horrible events of Friday night had happened a lifetime ago. Lucy and Hannah spent part of their morning assembling the spooky house, before setting it carefully on a back table in the kitchen to dry completely. Once the icing seams that held it together had hardened, they could begin attaching candies and piping spiderwebs in the corners.

Lucy had unpackaged some marshmallow ghosts that she planned to position around the house, setting them in a bowl, but Betsy kept sneaking into the kitchen to nibble on them.

"Betsy!" Lucy mock-scolded her. "What am I going to use for the landscaping if you eat all my ghosts?"

Betsy immediately looked guilty, and Lucy laughed. "Just kidding, knock yourself out. Aunt Tricia bought too many, anyway. We couldn't possibly use them all."

Hannah munched on candy corn and shook her head. "You can keep those marshmallow spooks. These, here, are my weakness. Candy corn and mallow-creme pumpkins!" She returned to her workbench with a handful of candy and flipped through the recipe book. "I just love Halloween."

Lucy grinned. *What was not to love about a holiday whose traditions included eating candy and dressing up?*

Aunt Tricia peeked her head around the corner. "Lucy, that reporter guy just parked in our lot. I think he's coming in."

Lucy frowned and untied her apron, intending to send Mr. Billings packing. She walked out front, but then hesitated, struck by a sudden thought. Bob Billings had been inside the Haunted Forest for hours on Friday night. *He may have seen something that would clear Derek's name.*

Deciding she would catch more bees with honey than vinegar, she plastered a pleasant expression on her face, and was standing behind the counter when the reporter came through the door.

"Hello, Mr. Billings," Lucy greeted him cordially.

He looked a bit startled at the warm reception. "Yes, um, hello!" He walked slowly toward the counter, seeming a little unsure of himself.

"Did you get your camera back from the police yet?" Lucy asked.

The man frowned, looking annoyed. "No. This town's police department doesn't seem to understand that I need my equipment to make a living. It's not like I have a spare, high quality camera lying around."

Lucy nodded sympathetically. "Well, maybe by the end of the day. What can I do for you?"

Mr. Billings nervously adjusted his glasses, peering at Lucy through magnified lenses. "Well, Ms. Hale, instead of doing a story on Sweet Delights Bakery, I'm planning to do a story on the town of Ivy Creek. I'm looking for some feedback from different shop owners and residents."

Lucy raised her brows. "Feedback on…?"

He cleared his throat and flicked invisible lint from his sleeve. "May I purchase a coffee, please? I'll be happy to sit and discuss the angle with you."

Lucy hesitated for a split second. Whatever the man's angle was, she had a hunch she wasn't going to like it. But she'd really like to question him about what he may have seen…

She turned to pour him a coffee. "I can sit for a few minutes," she said, coming around the counter. "But I'd like to ask you a question or two, as well."

The reporter's face lit up. "Quid pro quo," he said admiringly. "OK."

They sat at a corner table and Mr. Billings added sugar to his coffee, stirring and tasting, and adding more sugar. Once he seemed satisfied, Lucy asked, "May I go first?"

"Absolutely," he replied, with a magnanimous air. He regarded her over his spectacles, waiting.

Lucy leaned forward. "When you were behind the scenes at the Haunted Forest, did you see anyone that looked to be in a hurry? Specifically, rushing by on foot?"

Mr. Billings pondered her question, a thoughtful look on his face. Suddenly, he straightened. "Yes!" he exclaimed.

Lucy waited, holding her breath.

"There was one fellow who rushed by me so quickly he almost knocked me flat," the man recounted. "Didn't even apologize." He sniffed in disdain. "Bad manners annoy me."

Lucy asked eagerly, "What did he look like?" She wondered if the description would fit Russ Leighton with his long, stringy hair.

"He was in costume," Mr. Billings said cryptically, locking eyes with her.

Silence stretched, and Lucy waited, but he didn't elaborate.

"Well, what costume was he wearing?" Lucy finally asked, her patience wearing thin.

He raised his cup to his lips. "Looked like a werewolf to me," he said. He sipped his coffee, a smug expression on his face.

Lucy frowned at the man. "Derek… needed to be somewhere else," she informed the reporter, wishing she could mention the note. "That's why he was in a hurry."

Bob Billings lifted a shoulder casually, showing indifference. "My turn," he said.

Lucy didn't think it was quite fair, but she had agreed to give her feedback on his "angle". She nodded stiffly for him to begin.

"Ivy Creek has had an awful lot of murders in the past few years," he began, watching for Lucy's reaction. He ticked them off on his fingers. "This one at the Haunted Forest, the Fairy Tale Fair murder this past summer. Before that, there was that famous author at the library… and six months earlier, the well-known director, Pete Jensen…"

Lucy's face was impassive. "Yes, I suppose we've been through a rough patch in this town," she acknowledged, wondering if it had been a mistake to talk with him. He'd given her nothing.

Mr. Billings looked calculating. "Even though the police in Ivy Creek claim to have solved these crimes, still… murders keep happening. You know what I think?" He raised his eyebrows, prompting a response.

Lucy frowned, compressing her lips. She shook her head.

Mr. Billings leaned forward. "I think these murders were never really solved. I think all the murders were the work of one criminal, and the police are covering it up, so as not to scare the public."

He whispered conspiratorially, his eyes large and eager behind thick lenses.

"I believe Ivy Creek has a serial killer in its midst."

12

Lucy scoffed. "That's preposterous! The police have confessions in all of those cases."

"So, they claim," Mr. Billings intoned darkly. He waggled his brows mysteriously.

Lucy stood up from the table. *What a waste of time.*

"Hey, you said you'd provide feedback for my story," Mr. Billings protested as Lucy turned to leave. "I need a quote."

Lucy spun back around. "OK. Here's your quote. *Lucy Hale of Sweet Delights Bakery has complete confidence that the police will solve the murder of Tony Newton... as they have a proven success rate and take the protection of Ivy Creek's citizens very seriously.*"

She turned and walked away, leaving Mr. Billings staring after her, a disgruntled expression on his face.

LUCY WALKED BACK into the kitchen, noticing Aunt Tricia's smirk as she passed her. *That man was just insufferable!*

The back door to the parking lot was open, and Hannah was nowhere in sight. Lucy approached the open door and looked out.

Her friend was cradling the black cat in her arms, scratching its head, while the feline closed its eyes in bliss.

Hannah looked up and smiled. "She likes me. I've decided to adopt her."

Lucy's heart warmed at the sight, and her unpleasant conversation with Bob Billings was forgotten. She tiptoed forward.

"Am I going to spook her?" she asked, her hand outstretched to pet the kitty's silky, ebony fur.

Hannah shook her head. "I don't think so. She seems to have realized people are friendly." She looked down at the animal tenderly. "I talked to my landlord last night. As long as I pay a pet deposit, he's fine with me having a cat."

Lucy smiled, addressing the feline. "You're one lucky girl, to have found Hannah, you know that?" She stroked her fingers gently across the sleek fur, and the cat purred in contentment.

Lucy remarked, "You're right. She's not spooky at all."

Hannah's face lit up. "Hey! I think that would be a great name for her."

"What?" Lucy asked, confused. The kitty peered up at Hannah, her green eyes curious.

"Spooky," Hannah clarified, and looked down at her new pet. "Spooky will be your name, since we found each other near Halloween. What do you think, girl?"

The kitty closed her eyes, purring noisily, seeming to approve of the choice.

Around mid-afternoon, Lucy decided they were caught up enough with baking that she had time to run into town. There were a few ingredients they were running low on, but really, she just wanted an excuse to stop by and see Taylor. She was anxious to know how the second interview with Derek had worked out, and if Bob Billings' camera had yielded any clues.

She decided to call first to make sure he'd have a few minutes to talk, and he suggested they meet at the deli near Bing's Grocery.

"I won't have time for a sit-down," he cautioned. "But I was going to send someone over to get me a sandwich, anyway. I haven't had time to eat lunch yet."

Lucy agreed, knowing Taylor well enough to realize he'd be working day and night until he solved the murder. She'd take whatever time he had to spend with her.

When she got to the deli, Taylor was waiting outside and gave her a quick hug. She drew back, looking worriedly into his face. He looked tired, with bags under his eyes from lack of sleep, and his hair stuck out every which way, a sure sign he'd been running his fingers through it in frustration.

"Any progress?" she asked, and he lifted a shoulder.

"No great leaps forward," he said. "So far, we haven't found anything of interest on Bob Billings' camera. Just a lot of pictures of the actors and sets."

They entered the deli together and joined the line. Lucy decided she'd get a salad to take back with her for dinner. Aunt Tricia would be out, meeting with her book club.

"How did it go with Derek?" she asked, her voice low. "Is he in trouble?"

Taylor glanced down at her, his face impassive. "I have to be honest with you, Lucy. We haven't eliminated him as a suspect."

Lucy drew back, surprised. "I thought you were on his side! You saw the note."

Taylor looked around, not wanting to attract attention. "I'm not saying I believe he's guilty. But we have to go where the evidence leads us." He kept his voice to a murmur. "So far, we've been unable to prove it was someone else who wrote that note. And Derek has a history of altercations with the victim."

Lucy was silent. Even though she'd just met Joseph's brother, she knew he wasn't capable of cold-blooded murder. *But how to convince Taylor?*

The line moved up. "What about Russ Leighton?" Lucy asked in a whisper.

"He's still a suspect, also," Taylor answered, and their turn came next.

The pair placed their order, and Taylor paid for them both. A few minutes later, they were stepping out onto the sidewalk.

"I hate to keep this so brief," Taylor said apologetically. "I really need to get back, though."

Lucy offered him a smile, though it didn't reach her eyes. "I understand completely," she said, and kissed him on the cheek.

"Officer!"

A loud voice hailed Taylor, and he and Lucy swiveled around. It was Carl Marconi, a deep frown on his face. The man closed the distance between them in a few quick strides.

"Is there any progress on the investigation?" he demanded. "I haven't received any word."

Taylor answered smoothly. "As soon as we have news, you'll be the first to know, Mr. Marconi. We have your contact information."

The man's eyes flashed. "How many detectives are working on this case? There should be some progress by now. I'm losing money every day, you know!"

Taylor made a visible effort to keep his temper in check. "Mr. Marconi, we have put all available resources-"

"What about Willie Childers?" Mr. Marconi interrupted. "Have you questioned him?"

Taylor frowned. "Was Mr. Childers at the Haunted Forest on Friday night?"

Mr. Marconi scoffed. "Oh, he's too smart for that. But are you aware he had employees distributing flyers in my lot that night? Flyers advertising the House of Horrors, tucked under the wipers of cars, parked at *my* attraction!" The man was working himself up to a full-blown tantrum, and Lucy took a step back.

Taylor raised his eyebrows. "Are you wanting to file charges for trespassing?" His tone was even. "You'll have to come down to the station for that."

Mr. Marconi looked at him incredulously. "Trespassing? No." He shook his head in disgust. "What I want is for you to investigate him for murder!"

Taylor regarded him, expressionless, as the man continued.

"Willie Childers should be your number one suspect! Out of anyone, he had the most to gain. By shutting down my attraction, he's earning hundreds of dollars more every single night!"

Mr. Marconi narrowed his eyes at Taylor. "If that's not a motive for murder, I don't know what is."

13

Carl Marconi's words kept running through Lucy's mind, all through the afternoon and well into the evening.

She tossed and turned in her bed, wondering if Willie Childers could somehow have orchestrated the murder as a way to eliminate his competition. Money was often the motive in murder, and she had no doubt that Mr. Childers was now profiting from Tony Newton's death.

She finally got to sleep just before midnight, but by three a.m. her stomach woke her up, growling insistently. Her mid-afternoon salad was all she'd eaten for dinner, and now she was paying for skipping a meal. She decided to get up and have a quick snack.

Throwing on a robe, she made her way down the hallway and rounded the corner to the kitchen–and crashed right into Aunt Tricia, who shrieked loud enough to wake the dead, scaring Lucy to death, and sending Gigi scampering away.

"Oh, my goodness," Lucy held a hand to her racing heart. "You scared me!"

Aunt Tricia laughed shakily, leaning against the wall. "Not half as much as you scared me! I was already unable to sleep, imagining all sorts of sounds in the house. I made myself get up to double check the locks on all the doors and windows."

Lucy frowned, alarmed. After all, there was still a murderer on the loose. "What did you hear?"

Aunt Tricia waved a hand dismissively and sank into a kitchen chair. "Scratching of claws on the window… the rustling of bat wings. Foolishness," she admitted sheepishly.

Lucy took the chair across from her, studying her aunt's tired face. "Ah, yes, you're reading Dracula, aren't you?" She wondered if that was a wise choice, considering that the reality in Ivy Creek was scary enough at present.

Aunt Tricia nodded with a sigh. "Too late to change books now. The whole group is a quarter of the way through. My own fault, thinking horror would be a good seasonal choice. I guess I should have gone with Wuthering Heights or something."

Lucy consoled her. "Well, you'll be done with it soon enough. Just try not to let it get stuck in your subconscious." She stood and rummaged through the refrigerator, finding a slice of cold pizza.

Grabbing a napkin and a bottle of water, she headed for her bedroom, calling over her shoulder, "Good night, Auntie. Try to get some sleep!"

Aunt Tricia nodded and looked around the brightly lit kitchen, deciding to turn on some lights in the rest of the house, too. Maybe then she'd be able to fall asleep.

THE NEXT MORNING, Lucy pulled into a parking space in front of the five and dime, intending to make a quick stop to pick up some black licorice. This seemed to be the only place in town that carried it, and she'd miscalculated how much she'd need to decorate the roof of the spooky house.

Of course, as soon as she got inside, her imagination took over. She stood in the penny candy section, debating on using orange candy slices to build the edible chimney. *And maybe Reese's Pieces would look cute used as a walkway...*

So distracted was she, she wasn't aware of the conversation in the next aisle until one of the participants grew louder and more insistent.

"It was an inside job, I tell you!" A man's voice was raised, emphasizing his point. "Mark my words, next year Carl Marconi will be using this to his advantage. He'll be able to advertise a *real* Haunted Forest–the site of an unsolved murder!"

A second voice murmured agreement, adding, "Also, I'm sure he had some kind of insurance in place that's going to kick in now, to compensate him for loss of revenue. He'll probably wind up taking in more than he'd ever had made on ticket sales."

Lucy frowned, disagreeing with the cynical viewpoint. She believed Mr. Marconi's distress over having to shut down his attraction was genuine. Although… there may be some truth in the fact that the murder would attract even more customers next year.

People were funny like that, she mused. *Eager to stand in places where horrendous acts had once occurred.*

DOUGH SHALL NOT MURDER

Lucy tried to tune out their conversation and focus on her candy choices. She really needed to get over to the bakery.

Suddenly, she heard a familiar voice. "You fellas are way off base. I was there that night, and you guys weren't. I'm pretty sure I saw the murderer, and it wasn't no inside job, either. This fellow wasn't someone who worked there."

Shocked, Lucy stood on tiptoe and peeked over the top shelf into the next aisle.

Russ Leighton was standing with two men she'd never seen before, lecturing them.

"He was wearing a long black coat, like a trench coat, and I saw him sneak into the forest when no one was watching, all furtive-like."

One of the other men looked skeptical. "Oh, yeah? What did this guy look like, exactly?"

Russ shook his head, his long hair swinging over his shoulders. "I couldn't see his face that clearly; cause he was wearing a hood. But I know everyone that worked there, and I didn't know this guy."

Lucy stood wide-eyed, transfixed by the disclosure. *Was Russ telling the truth? Maybe he really had seen something. After all, the killer would need a long coat to conceal the murder weapon.*

The other man laughed. "You saw someone in a long, black cape with a hood walk into the Haunted Forest... news flash, man. That was an actor. Half of them over there wear long, black capes."

Russ frowned, stubbornly insisting, "It wasn't anyone who worked there! And it wasn't a cape. It was a long coat with a

Betsy peered at her hopefully. "Have you heard anything from Taylor?'

Lucy shook her head. "He said there's been no real progress." She thought of sharing what she'd just overheard, but she didn't want to give Betsy false hope. Best to tell Taylor first and see what became of it.

Aunt Tricia looked a bit peaked, and Lucy studied her face with concern. "Did you get any sleep, Auntie?"

The older woman smiled ruefully. "I managed to drop off around dawn. And dreamed there was a coffin in our cellar." She shook her head. "I guess I was blessed with a strong imagination."

Lucy suggested, "Maybe you should take the day off? Go home and catch up on your sleep? We can handle the bakery today. I doubt it will be too busy."

Aunt Tricia tilted her head, considering. "I can't say that's not tempting. I might just leave at noon, then. I want to at least be here for the morning rush."

They heard the back door of the kitchen open just then, and Hannah called out a greeting. A minute later, she appeared in the archway behind the counter, with a satisfied grin on her face.

"Did you take Spooky home last night?" asked Lucy, noting her friend's good mood.

"Oh, I love that name!" exclaimed Betsy, while Hannah nodded.

"I sure did. And she seems to be settling in like a champ. The only problem was this morning. She wanted to go outside, but I need to wait until after our vet visit in a few weeks.

Also, I want her to recognize my house is home, so she won't get lost trying to make her way back here."

"I'm so glad you adopted that sweet little kitty," Aunt Tricia said approvingly. "With winter on the way, especially."

The talk turned to business next, with Lucy outlining which items to put on special, and Betsy noting them on the chalkboard for the patrons to see. Hannah tied on an apron and disappeared into the kitchen to begin baking. Soon, the wonderful aroma of apples and cinnamon filled the air, riding on fragrant waves from the back room.

The bell jangled, and Joseph walked in, causing Betsy to break into a grin. She came around the counter for a quick embrace, kissing his cheek.

"It smells so good in here!" Joseph commented. "Is that apple pie?"

"Close… apple turnovers." Hannah appeared in the archway, wiping her hands on a towel. "Hi, Joseph. How's Derek?"

Joseph sighed and rubbed at his face. "Pretty down," he admitted. "Maybe I'll grab a few pastries to bring home, to cheer him up. He's staying with me for the time being."

Betsy asked, "Do you want to sit for a minute? I can bring you a coffee…"

He nodded and made his way over to a table close to the counter. Betsy poured him a cup of strong brew and added a freshly baked turnover to a small plate, setting it before him.

"Careful now, they're piping hot," she murmured, resting a hand on his shoulder.

"This is great. Thanks." He looked up and offered her a smile. Betsy patted his shoulder and went back to her tasks behind the counter.

Lucy eased into a chair across from him, wishing she could take the worry from his face. *Maybe the information Russ had will pan out*, she thought hopefully.

"I have a bit of a dilemma," Joseph disclosed, breaking open the steaming pastry.

Lucy raised her brows inquisitively, regarding her friend.

"The production..." he sighed and looked worried, continuing. "Specifically, who should play the lead. Although opening night is still five weeks away, it needs to be cast now, so we can begin rehearsals."

Lucy frowned. "Why wouldn't Derek..." she stopped, and Joseph met her gaze.

"He *would* be the perfect choice. He already knows the part. But with him under suspicion for murder–the murder of the former lead, no less–I don't think it would be well received by the public for the theater to cast him as Arthur."

He looked pensive, picking apart the flaky pastry crust. "Actually, it might be better to cancel the production entirely. I'm not sure the town will come flocking to the theater with an unsolved murder hanging over us."

Lucy was silent, seeing his point. *Poor Derek, and poor Joseph! Derek would be denied a role he deserved because of an unfounded suspicion. And Joseph's hard work might be all for naught. That was some tough luck.*

"Who knows, Joseph?" she said, rising from the table, unable to offer any solution. "It could be the investigation will catch a break soon."

Joseph nodded and sipped his coffee. "I'm hopeful," he said, but he didn't look it.

Lucy returned to the counter, eyeing the phone. *Why hadn't Taylor called yet?* She was tempted to drive over there, but she knew he was up to his ears in work.

Behind her, the bell jangled, and she turned to welcome the new customer. Aunt Tricia and Betsy had gone upstairs to prepare the veranda for customers.

The greeting died on her lips as she blinked in surprise at the man who had entered the bakery. His large frame appeared dark and ominous against the bright morning light streaming through the windows.

It was Willie Childers, his coat buttoned against the crisp air of the new day.

Lucy's heart thumped madly as she stared, wide-eyed, at the garment.

Mr. Childers wore a long, black, hooded coat with a row of buttons marching down the front.

15

"Do you sell donuts?" Mr. Childers barked out, pinning Lucy with a hard-eyed gaze. His expression wasn't any more pleasant than the last time she'd seen him, arguing with Carl Marconi.

"Uh... donuts? No," Lucy managed to answer, still looking wide-eyed at the man's coat.

Mr. Childers blew out a breath in disgust. "What kind of bakery doesn't have donuts?" He grumbled and turned on his heel. The bell jangled loudly as he stomped out the door.

Aunt Tricia and Betsy came around the corner just then.

"What was that about?" Aunt Tricia asked, a frown on her face. Mr. Childers stood on the sidewalk in front of the bakery, hands on his hips, scanning the street.

Lucy took a deep breath. *She needed to talk to Taylor now!*

"Nothing." She waved a hand dismissively, not ready to share her suspicions. "Apparently, he's looking for donuts." She headed for the staircase, deciding she would give Taylor another call. "I'll be in my office for a few minutes. Nice to see you, Joseph," she called out.

Upstairs, Lucy sat at her desk and dialed Taylor's cell phone number. She hated to bug him, but this couldn't wait. Thankfully, this time he answered.

"Hey, Lucy, I'm sorry I hadn't called you back yet," Taylor said, seeing the bakery on his caller I.D.

"That's OK, I know you're busy. Taylor, I overheard something this morning…" Lucy launched into the story of what she'd heard Russ say in the five and dime this morning.

He listened attentively, with the occasional "hmm", until she'd finished.

"Well, that does bear looking into," he said, his tone thoughtful. "Funny how Russ didn't bring that up while he was in here. You do realize, though, Lucy, that if Russ were the killer, he might spread a story like that, just to take suspicion off himself."

Lucy frowned. She hadn't thought of that. "Hmm. Yes, I suppose so. But Taylor, guess who walked into the bakery just now, wearing a long, hooded, black coat with buttons?"

"Who?"

"Willie Childers!" Lucy announced. "And he had motive, more than anyone else, to put the Haunted Forest out of business."

"Well," Taylor's tone was bemused. "That's interesting. But Mr. Childers didn't have the opportunity to steal the sword from the theater. And forensics has confirmed that the sword was the murder weapon."

Lucy was stumped. *How would Mr. Childers have obtained the sword?*

"You know," she said slowly, "Mr. Childers does employ a lot of young actors at the House of Horrors. Maybe one of them tried out for the play. He might have bribed someone to swipe the sword for him."

Taylor sighed. "That's possible. And it's also possible that Russ is spreading the story, Lucy. Especially if he knew Mr. Childers owns a long, black coat. Either way, I'll be bringing Russ in for another round of questioning. Thanks for the heads up. I'll keep you posted."

They exchanged goodbyes, and Lucy hung up the phone, pondering the possibilities. She walked back downstairs and found Aunt Tricia and Betsy waiting on a pair of women, one of whom had a toddler in tow. Joseph had apparently gone on his way. Lucy smiled a greeting at the customers as she passed by, heading into the kitchen.

Hannah was working on the edible spooky house, using royal icing to add sticks of orange-striped chewing gum alongside the windows for shutters. The house itself was about half-decorated.

"What do you think?" Hannah asked, looking up from her work. Her eyes were sparkling, and Lucy's mood lifted perceptibly. Halloween was a fun holiday in the bakery.

"Looks great!" Lucy told her. She decided to help, mixing a bit of food coloring into a bowl of icing.

She'd need some "dirt" for the landscaping, so she tinted the icing a light brown. She and Hannah would make a graveyard, using small cookies shaped as tombstones, and add marshmallow ghosts and candy pumpkins.

"Are you and Taylor going to carve pumpkins together?" Hannah asked, refilling her pastry bag.

Lucy spread some "graveyard dirt" on the board, carefully avoiding the front walkway Hannah had created with Reese's Pieces candy.

"Yes, probably," she answered distractedly.

She hadn't really thought about it, but Halloween was coming up fast. She'd been so caught up in the case, she'd yet to watch a single scary movie. *Probably just as well*, she thought. Aunt Tricia was spooked enough, just reading Dracula. Scary movies on TV in their living room wouldn't help.

As if summoned, Aunt Tricia poked her head around the corner.

"Any more pumpkin muffins back here?" she asked Hannah. Her eyes fell on the spooky house, and she smiled with delight.

"That's looking great, girls!" she commended them. "I can't wait to see the little kids' faces once it's all set up in the front window."

Lucy grinned. "It should be ready in a day or two."

Hannah nodded, stepping back to eye her work. She glanced at Aunt Tricia. "Pumpkin muffins? Yes, there's a dozen more on the cooling rack."

As her aunt gathered up a few of the pastries, Lucy glanced at the clock. "Auntie, aren't you just doing a half a day today?"

Aunt Tricia nodded. "I'm just stocking up the front case for Betsy, then I'll be going." She headed back toward the front as the bell jangled. "It's Mrs. White," she stage-whispered, peeking out.

Hannah looked over at Lucy and uttered a mock groan. "There go all my pumpkin muffins!"

Lucy chuckled. Mrs. White was their best customer, coming in several times per week to buy desserts and assorted treats for her large family. She was also known to talk your ear off.

"I'll help Betsy," she told her aunt, putting down her spatula. "You go on home and get some rest."

Lucy washed her hands quickly at the sink, knowing that if Mrs. White managed to engage Aunt Tricia in conversation, the poor dear wouldn't be able to leave for twenty minutes.

She walked through the archway, and Mrs. White spotted her, giving Aunt Tricia a moment to escape. Her aunt caught Lucy's eye and winked, slipping out the door.

"Lucy!" the woman crowed, as if she hadn't seen her in a month. "How are you, dear?"

Lucy smiled. "Hi, Mrs. White. What can we get for you today?"

The woman pursed her lips, scanning the bakery case. She pointed to a new item.

"Those look good. What are they?" She peered at the small notecard.

"Pumpkin chess bars," Lucy replied. "They're like little squares of pumpkin pie on a shortbread crust."

"Very yummy!" Betsy chimed in.

"Oh, yes, let's do that," Mrs. White decided, looking pleased. "Could I have a dozen, please. Oh, no, make that sixteen. And two of those peach turnovers, too. No, better make it three."

As Betsy removed trays from the case and began boxing up the woman's order, Mrs. White set her oversized purse on the counter. It was the size of a large tote bag, and she unpacked items from it in search of her wallet.

She pulled a rolled-up newspaper from the bag, asking Lucy, "Could you put this in your recycle, if you don't mind? I've already checked my horoscope. It's just taking up space."

Lucy nodded. "Sure." She set the paper down on the telephone counter behind her and turned back to accept Mrs. White's credit card.

A few minutes later, the transaction was complete, and a happy Mrs. White was taking her leave, nodding gaily from the door, her arms laden with boxes. The bell jangled as she let herself out.

"Whew!" joked Betsy, and Lucy laughed.

For a visit from Mrs. White, they had escaped unscathed. The woman was notorious for buying out their entire stock of items. Thankfully, they had backup pumpkin chess bars in the walk-in cooler.

"What are the damages?" asked Hannah, with a grin, emerging from the kitchen.

"Not too bad," replied Lucy. "We may need more pumpkin chess bars by the end of the day."

Hannah nodded. "Not a problem." She spotted the newspaper by the telephone. "Hey, what's this?" She unfolded the paper to read the headline.

"Holy moly, Lucy, did you see this?" Shocked, Hannah spread the paper out on the front counter for Lucy and Betsy to read.

It was The Ivy Creek Voice, a second-rate newspaper known mostly for its horoscopes and sensationalistic stories. The headline on the front page screamed out in bold, black letters.

A REAL MONSTER LURKS IN THE HAUNTED FOREST

Below that, even more disturbing, was the subheading:

Zombie Actor Murdered, Slashed by Sword

16

Shocked, Lucy zeroed in on the byline.

Bob Billings.

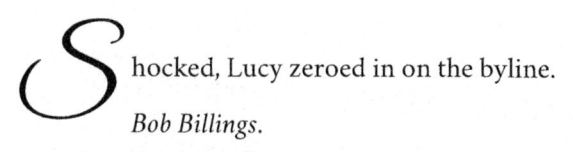

"I thought the murder weapon was being kept under wraps," Hannah commented, a frown on her face.

"How did that reporter find out?" Betsy asked in a hushed voice.

How, indeed, Lucy wondered, scanning the article. The news story reported that a young actor was found murdered at the Haunted Forest on Friday night, his body left lying across the trail.

How did Bob Billings know where the body had been found?

Hannah looked up, having read the same line. "Uh-oh. Maybe there's a leak at the Ivy Creek police department."

Lucy sighed, knowing Taylor would not be happy about this. She'd have to tell him. If he'd already seen the article, he would have mentioned it on the phone.

"I guess there could be..." she answered absently, her thoughts whirling. Russ Leighton suddenly popped into her mind. *Had he spoken to Bob Billings? Russ knew about the sword.*

Lucy decided she'd better call over to the station. She wasn't sure if she'd reach Taylor, but she needed to let him know about the article, even if she had to leave a message.

Just as she reached for the phone, it rang, and she drew back, startled. Rolling her eyes at her own jumpiness, she picked up the receiver.

"Sweet Delights Bakery," she said automatically. "How may I help you?"

"Is this Lucy?"

Lucy frowned, not quite recognizing the voice. "It is, yes."

"This is Bob Billings. You remember, the reporter who-"

Lucy blinked in surprise before cutting him off. "Yes, I know who you are, Mr. Billings. I've actually just seen your article in The Ivy Creek Voice." Her tone was censuring.

The man seemed oblivious to her disapproval, responding enthusiastically, "Yes, my front-page story! What did you think?"

Lucy was silent for a moment, wondering if she should just let Taylor handle this. The temptation to find out the facts for herself was too strong, however, and she plunged forward.

"Mr. Billings... could you tell me how you came by the information you quoted? I don't believe the police have released any such details, like the murder weapon, or where the body was found."

There was silence for a moment, and then Mr. Billings replied cryptically, "I have an inside source who was at the scene."

"At the scene," Lucy repeated. "But when?"

If someone had witnessed the body laying across the trail, they may have seen the murderer.

On the heels of that thought came another.

If that person had seen the body, why hadn't they called the police?

Mr. Billings replied stiffly, "Right after the murder occurred." His tone was brisk. "Listen, I'm not giving up any more details. I protect my sources." As Lucy pondered his response, he added, "Anyway, that's not why I called your bakery."

"Why *did* you call?" Lucy countered, frustrated with the man's secretiveness.

"I decided to give you another chance to be in my article," he replied loftily. "You've been involved in several of the murder investigations in Ivy Creek. It's rather odd, actually, how you always seem to be at the center of these incidents." He sounded jealous, and Lucy grimaced with annoyance, ready to hang up. But he wasn't finished.

"I think you should realize, Ms. Hale, that when I run my story about a serial killer in Ivy Creek, I plan to mention how you always seem to be mixed up in the cases. I think it will look odd if you don't comment. The readers might feel like you're trying to hide something." His smug tone of voice grated on her nerves, and Lucy fought the urge to slam down the phone.

"I believe you're underestimating the residents of Ivy Creek," she replied coolly. "They're not so easily led. And if you think back, Mr. Billings, you might remember, I did give you a quote." Lucy hung up the phone, still bristling.

"What did he say?" Hannah asked, noticing Lucy's ire. Betsy stood beside her, looking alarmed.

"He wouldn't name his source," Lucy answered, exasperated. "Maybe Taylor can get some answers out of him. The man obviously knows more than he should about the case."

Hannah looked around the empty bakery. "Maybe you should head over to see Taylor now," she suggested. "You know you're just going to stew about this until you tell him."

Lucy tilted her head, considering. It would probably be pretty slow from here on out. She knew Betsy and Hannah could manage for an hour without her.

"OK, you're right," she said. She picked up a bakery box. "I might as well bring the fellas some treats. They're going to need a pick-me-up, the way they've been working around the clock."

Twenty minutes later, Lucy was walking into the Ivy Creek Police Department, with her trademark pink and black bakery box. She was greeted by cheers from the officers in the main room.

She grinned, setting the box down, and looked up to see Taylor walking her way.

"What a nice surprise," he said, kissing her on the cheek. He eyed the open box.

Lucy smiled indulgently. "Better grab a pastry before they're gone, and then I have some news for you."

Taylor selected a salted caramel cookie and Lucy followed him into his private office with the offending newspaper rolled up and tucked under her arm.

Taylor rested a hip on his desk. "I was just about to call you," he said, munching on the cookie. "I finished interviewing Russ Leighton fifteen minutes ago."

Lucy was tempted to ask about the interview first, but she'd rather get the unpleasant news over with. "Taylor, Mrs. White brought this into the bakery." She laid the paper out on his desk.

Taylor hovered over the newspaper, his face darkening with anger as he read the headline. He set the cookie down on his blotter, and picked the paper up, studying it.

"How did this get out? We were trying to keep that information under wraps!"

Lucy knew his question was rhetorical, but she shook her head, sympathizing.

"I talked to Bob Billings after I saw this," she offered. "He happened to call right when I'd finished reading it. He claims to have an inside source."

Taylor huffed with displeasure. "That source better not be one of my men." He tapped the paper on the edge of the desk thoughtfully. "Whoever gave these details to Mr. Billings needs to come forward. It could be they have evidence crucial to this case."

"Maybe you'll have better luck getting a name out of Bob Billings." Lucy's tone was cynical. She changed the subject, asking, "What happened with Russ Leighton? Did he tell you anything more? Did he mention Mr. Childers?"

Taylor shook his head, his lips compressed. "Russ's memory of Friday night is pretty spotty. His information contradicts itself. First, he told me he saw the man in the long, black coat early on, way before he got into the argument with Chris at the gate. Then he changed his story and said it was after I told him to go home. When I pointed out the discrepancy, he admitted he has some holes in his memory from that night."

Lucy frowned. "What do you mean, holes in his memory?"

Taylor looked grim. "He's an alcoholic, Lucy. He has blackouts, where he can't remember big chunks of time. Sometimes, he can't remember how he's gotten from point A to point B. For instance, he was picked up sleeping in the parking lot of Big Lou's Bar and Grill, but he doesn't remember leaving the Haunted Forest."

Lucy looked at him in alarm. "That sounds pretty dangerous. Do you think he might have killed Tony and blacked it out?"

Taylor looked noncommittal, but his expression was serious. "It's a possibility, Lucy. He had motive, and the opportunity to steal the sword from the theater. And now, he's admitting to frequent blackouts." His eyes locked with hers.

"Are you holding him?" Lucy's voice was barely more than a whisper. She'd not viewed Russ as a threat before, but now...

Taylor shook his head. "We don't have enough evidence to charge him yet. And we're still investigating other suspects," he reminded her.

Lucy nodded, her thoughts far away. She replayed Friday night in her head, and the way Russ had stood at the edge of the parking lot, gazing into the forest after Taylor had told him to leave. She shivered.

Had Russ been plotting Tony's murder at that very moment, his conscience dulled by alcohol, with misguided vengeance fueling his actions?

17

"*Easy*, now, watch the threshold..." Lucy cautioned Hannah, who was walking backward.

Together, they were carrying their masterpiece–the edible spooky house, which had been completed the day before and left to dry overnight. Betsy stood by the reserved spot at the front window, waiting excitedly, while Aunt Tricia wrung her hands anxiously, and offered helpful advice.

"Almost there, another ten feet. Watch the chair! OK... there you go!"

Hannah grinned as she and Lucy lowered the board holding the festive structure to the recessed window area.

"Whew! That was nerve-wracking!"

Lucy withdrew the battery-operated light from her apron pocket and switched it on, flicking through the settings. She settled on a glow that grew softly and then ebbed away, on a repeat loop.

"Here we go," she said, scooting the board out a bit to access the cutout hidden beneath the house. She popped the light inside, and the butterscotch candy windows glowed a spooky orange. Lucy eyed the house critically, carefully positioning it to the best advantage for street viewing.

"Let's go look!" Betsy suggested, and the crew trundled outside. Lucy flipped off the bakery lights at the doorway to better see the effect.

Their Halloween window dressing was now complete. The spooky house rested in the center, stealing the show, resplendent with fall-colored candies, and little marshmallow ghosts. Fake fall leaves were scattered around the base, and tiny, festive, pumpkin-shaped lights twinkled above in loopy strands. Ghosts and a red-eyed bat were hung from wires above the house, completing the picture.

Aunt Tricia smiled at the sight and turned to Lucy and Hannah.

"I think that's the best Halloween window ever," she said. "Well done, ladies!"

Betsy gazed at the lit-up house with a child's fascination. "I can't wait for Joseph to see this!"

Hannah shivered as a brisk breeze kicked up. "Let's go inside. It's too chilly for me out here!"

As they entered the bakery, Lucy asked Betsy, "So, has Joseph said anything about the production? Is he going to have to cancel?"

Betsy rounded the corner and began to make herself a hot chocolate. She looked over her shoulder at Lucy with a smile and good news.

"The show is back on! Joseph talked to Derek, and Derek convinced him to go ahead with casting a new lead. He doesn't want Joseph to catch any backlash, so he's going to step down from the running."

"What an admirable young man," Aunt Tricia commented. "Thinking of the theater's success before his own."

Betsy nodded, her smile slipping away. "I do wish this whole thing was over with. I hate that Derek is still considered a suspect. Anyone who's ever met him knows he could never be responsible for that awful murder!" She shuddered at the memory.

Hannah remarked, "Well, I'll certainly sleep better once the police solve the case. It gives me the heebie jeebies thinking that the killer might still be walking around in our little town."

"When are the tryouts for the new lead?" Lucy asked, curious. She knew Joseph wanted to get things rolling. They'd already wasted almost a week.

"Tomorrow, all day long," Betsy answered. She looked a little worried. "Joseph's afraid there won't be much turnout. It's such short notice. Derek tacked up an announcement at the college, but I'm not sure what else we can do."

Lucy had a sudden thought. "Hey! Maybe Sweet Delights could provide muffins. You know college students, always hungry. They'll turn up for free food."

Betsy grinned. "That's a great idea! If you don't mind..."

Lucy waved her hand. "Of course not. Joseph is a good friend."

Hannah gave a mock groan, tying on her apron. "Just when I thought my work was done…"

Lucy laughed and poked her. "I'll help. We'll get it done in no time."

Betsy sighed happily. "I'm going to call and let Joseph know. Maybe Derek can add that to the announcement."

Lucy nodded, donning her apron, and headed into the kitchen.

Lucy arrived at the theater at nine sharp the next morning. The small parking lot had at least a half dozen cars already, and she was cheered by the sight. It was still early. Maybe the amended flyer would help the turnout, after all.

She shouldered her way in through the door, carrying the box full of muffins, and had to stop for a minute, blinking, while her eyes adjusted to the dim lighting. Auditions had begun at eight, and there was an actor on the stage reading from a script.

Lucy made her way quietly over to a table set up to the side and began to arrange her muffins on the platter Joseph had set out. As she completed her task, the reading concluded, and there was a short burst of applause. She turned her head to see Joseph approach the stage and speak briefly with the actor, before he turned to the rest of the candidates, seated in the audience.

"A short break, ten minutes, and we'll hear from Fred Freeman next." He caught sight of Lucy at the back of the theater. "Sweet Delights Bakery has generously provided us with some breakfast pastries, so get yours while they last."

The small crowd of college aged individuals swiveled their heads as one, an excited buzz of conversation escalating as they rose from their seats. Lucy stepped off to one side as she saw Joseph approach.

"How's it going?" she asked. "Looks like a pretty good turnout for this early."

Joseph seemed pleased, nodding his head. "I have to say, advertising free pastries might have done the trick. Thanks so much, Lucy! I owe you one."

Lucy smiled, glad to see the worry lines gone from her friend's face for the moment. "How's Derek holding up?"

Joseph looked pensive. "Well, he's not talking about it much, but it may be good that he's trying to focus on other things. There's really nothing we can do besides let the police investigate."

Lucy nodded, wishing there was more she could do. Her gaze flickered back to the crowd at the refreshment table, landing on a familiar form. She narrowed her eyes.

"Is that Bob Billings?" The question was rhetorical. She could clearly see the reporter, his camera once again looped around his neck, pouring himself a cup of coffee from the dispenser.

Joseph glanced that way and nodded. "He's putting together a book about the history of the theater. He's probably taken about a hundred photos so far. Mostly of the old architecture."

Lucy was bemused. A coffee table book... that didn't seem to be the reporter's style. She shook her head, reminding herself she really didn't know the man at all.

"Well, I better get over to the bakery," she told Joseph, looking at her watch. "You should drop by and see our Halloween window. We set up the spooky house yesterday."

Joseph grinned. "Betsy mentioned that! We're planning to stop by after dinner in town tonight. She said after dark will be the best time to see it."

Lucy grinned, thinking of Betsy's childlike wonder. It was refreshing to be around.

"Great! Say hello to Derek," she said, turning to leave. "And good luck with the auditions."

"Thank you. I will," promised Joseph. "I know all this mess will be behind us soon." He raised his eyes to the heavens. "It has to be."

As she left the dimly lit theater and stepped back out into the sunshine, Lucy took a deep breath, hoping fervently that Joseph was right.

18

"It's simple. All you do is place two Junior Mints like this," Lucy instructed, setting the candies one on top of the other, on the surface of the piping hot sugar cookies.

"Press down slightly. Then, add one mini chocolate chip for each ear..." Lucy positioned the chocolates above the top Junior Mint. "And three more here, for the tail."

Betsy watched eagerly. "Is that all?"

"Not quite," Lucy chuckled at the young woman's enthusiasm. "Wait a minute for the heat of the cookies to melt the mini chocolate chips, then take a skewer and smudge the chocolate. Into points for the ears." She demonstrated. "And into a line for the tail."

Betsy looked down at the black cat sugar cookie, her face wreathed in smiles. "That's so adorable!" She looked at her employer. "Can I do the rest?"

Lucy nodded, teasing, "Sure. But don't eat all the Junior Mints! Or you won't have enough for the cats."

Hannah watched, amused, as Betsy began to carefully position mints for the cats' heads and bodies. "If the cookies get too cool to melt the chocolate, just pop them back in the oven for a minute," she advised.

The front door jangled open, and Aunt Tricia appeared in the kitchen doorway moments later. "Oh, there you are, Betsy! I see Lucy has you making the black cat cookies." The older woman smiled nostalgically. "That's been a Sweet Delights Bakery tradition for twenty-five years, at least!"

Betsy looked up, awe on her face. "Your mother made these?" She asked Lucy.

Lucy nodded with a fond smile. "One of my earliest memories of helping Mom in the bakery was standing on a step stool and portioning out the mints and chocolate chips for each cookie. I was too young to place them on the cookies–Mom was afraid I'd touch the hot pan and get burned." She chuckled. "I probably ate more Junior Mints than I portioned out, though!"

Aunt Tricia smiled, resting a loving hand on Lucy's shoulder. "I remember those days. One of your other favorite cookies to help her with was the jack-o'-lanterns. Do you remember?"

Lucy nodded, and Hannah spoke up from across the room. "We'll be making some of those later."

Betsy exclaimed, "Oh, I want to learn those, too!" She glanced at Aunt Tricia. "But, of course, if you need me out front…"

Aunt Tricia shook her head. "I can handle things out here until the lunch rush, Betsy. Go ahead and learn all the holiday cookies. I'm sure Lucy and Hannah could use your help."

Lucy nodded. "We've been selling out of most of our pumpkin-flavored items, so Hannah and I can catch up on that while Betsy concentrates on the Halloween cookies."

The three women worked companionably together in the kitchen, chatting about their own Halloween memories, and the morning passed swiftly. As the lunch rush began, Betsy went back behind the counter to help Aunt Tricia with the steady flow of customers. By one-thirty, the pace had slowed down, and Betsy popped her head back into the kitchen.

"I'm about to take a break, and I just realized that I never shared my photos of the Haunted Hayride." Her mouth twisted in a rueful expression. "I guess I was trying to put it all behind me, but I did see one or two photos that you guys might like… before all that other stuff happened."

Lucy perked up. "Oh, I'd love to see them!"

Hannah chimed in, agreeing, and Betsy grinned. "Let's go upstairs on the veranda. Tricia just returned from her break, so she told me to go take lunch. I have the photos on my Google account, but, Lucy, if you want to grab your laptop, we'll see them better than on the phone."

"Great idea," Lucy said, untying her apron. In the back of her mind, she wondered if Betsy might have caught anything unusual in her photos. It was worth a look.

The trio settled comfortably into the patio chairs upstairs, and Lucy powered up her laptop. Betsy took over, typing in her Google photos account information, and suddenly the screen was filled with their own happy faces.

They all laughed, peering first at the silly expressions Joseph made at Betsy, and Lucy smiled to see a candid shot of Taylor hugging her close while they waited in line.

The hayride pictures began next, and Betsy shuddered, looking at the scary scenes. "They did a phenomenal job with the settings and the actors' makeup," she commented. "Almost too real."

Hannah agreed, wincing when she saw her own face looking wide-eyed and alarmed. Betsy had captured the moment when the ghoul had clung to the wagon right beside her. "Oh, wow, I'd forgotten about that."

Betsy scrolled through the photos, with all of them chuckling, until she reached the scene of the vampire in the clearing, his arms raised as if about to take flight.

"Wait!" commanded Lucy, and Betsy stopped, looking at her inquisitively.

"What?" she sounded puzzled.

Lucy squinted at the screen and pointed to the upper right corner. "There… do you see what I see? Can you zoom in, Betsy?"

Betsy hit the zoom button and magnified the image, and the shadowy form of a man suddenly filled the screen. He appeared to be hiding behind one of the trees just outside of the clearing, and Lucy's eyes widened as she realized what she was seeing.

The man wore a long, hooded black coat. Shadows fell across his face, making him unrecognizable, but it was apparent from his posture that he had seen the wagon approaching and was trying to remain unnoticed.

Lucy heard Betsy gasp as she suddenly realized what she had inadvertently captured. The young woman turned to Lucy, her freckles standing out on her ashen face.

"Oh, my goodness! He looks like he's trying to hide. Do you think…?" Her voice trailed off and she gulped nervously.

Lucy nodded grimly, finishing Betsy's thought.

"I think you may have snapped a photo of the murderer."

19

Lucy wasted no time getting over to the Ivy Creek Police department. Within fifteen minutes, she was in Taylor's office, opening her laptop and pulling up the photo for him to examine.

They stared together at the shadowy figure pressed up against the tree.

"Can't really see his face, though," Taylor murmured thoughtfully. He scrolled through the rest of the pictures, but that was the only picture the mysterious person had appeared in.

He glanced up at Lucy. "You realize this rules out Willie Childers, though? If this is, indeed, a picture of the murderer."

Lucy frowned. "Why?"

He tapped the tree next to the figure. "Use the tree as a scale. This is a slender man who's not overly tall. Mr. Childers is rather large."

Lucy's eyes widened, realizing he was right. "It could still be Russ Leighton, though," she mused.

Taylor nodded. "It could be. Although, all we have, honestly, is a picture of someone who looks like they're trying to hide. There's no proof this is the murderer."

Lucy nodded. "What will you do next?"

Taylor scratched his chin, pondering. "I'll call in Carl Marconi and see if he recognizes the man in the photo. If he can rule out that it's an employee, then we'll go from there. Maybe the photo can be enhanced using digital software to clear it up a bit."

Lucy thought for a moment. "If it's not an employee, then it's almost certainly the murderer, because a customer wouldn't be allowed to walk into the forest on foot. They'd have to be on the hay wagon."

Taylor nodded. "Can you send me this photo?"

Lucy nodded and bent over the keyboard. With a few clicks, she sent the photo to Taylor's email.

He thanked her, giving her shoulder an affectionate squeeze, and Lucy packed up her laptop.

As she left his office, he called her name, and she turned back, seeing a worried look on his handsome face. "I know I don't have to tell you… but be careful, Lucy."

She smiled and nodded, reassuring him. "Always."

On her way back to the bakery, Lucy drove past Nelson's farm stand. Her attention was caught by their pumpkin patch, all decked out with a scarecrow and a ghost flying beneath the banner.

Why not pick up a few pumpkins right now? Maybe Taylor would catch a break in the case soon, and they'd be able to enjoy some Halloween activities together. Even if he wasn't free to carve jack-o'-lanterns with her this year, she and Aunt Tricia could carry on the tradition.

Lucy pulled into the parking lot and began to peruse the selection. She selected two pumpkins that were almost perfectly symmetrical and brought them up to the stand.

"Lucy Hale! I was wondering when you'd be in," the older woman behind the counter greeted her with a smile.

Lucy grinned. Her family had always bought their pumpkins from the Nelsons, and it was like stepping back in time to see Mrs. Nelson. She hadn't changed in all the years Lucy had known her, still wearing denim overalls, with her hair all bundled up under a colorful scarf.

She inquired after Mrs. Nelson's family, and they chatted for a minute about the bakery before concluding their transaction.

"Tell your Aunt Tricia hello for me," Mrs. Nelson said, before adding, "I do hope that reporter isn't pestering either of you too much."

Lucy cocked her head, frowning. "Bob Billings? Why do you say that?"

The woman narrowed her eyes, looking irritated. "He's been coming around town, bothering everyone who does business here, going on about a serial killer in Ivy Creek. Glorifying that horrible murder at The Haunted Forest. He told me you and your aunt refused to talk to him, and even had the audacity to imply you two were part of a police cover-up!" She sounded indignant.

Lucy scoffed. "He's come into the bakery twice, and yes, it's true that we won't give him fuel for his fire. How ridiculous, though!"

Mrs. Nelson nodded, her dark eyes flashing. "I want you to know, dear, that no one in town is listening to him. Every person I've talked to has sent him on his way as soon as he starts poking into all the misfortune we've had in the last few years. Ivy Creek's citizens aren't feeling too kindly toward him."

Lucy compressed her lips, shaking her head. "That's good to hear. But I know someone in town must feel differently. Mr. Billings had an article in The Ivy Creek Voice the other day, with a lot of privileged information in it. Things he wouldn't know on his own."

Mrs. Nelson waved her hand dismissively. "No one reads that rag, anyway." She looked up at the sky, saying, "Well, I better get Jonas to put the equipment away. Looks like some rain, headed our way." She waved goodbye as Lucy loaded the pumpkins into her SUV.

Lucy drove back to the bakery, mulling over the woman's words.

What would it take to make Bob Billings give up on this serial killer nonsense?

THE NEXT DAY, Aunt Tricia and Lucy were sitting at the breakfast table, enjoying a rare, leisurely morning. Betsy and Hannah were opening Sweet Delights alone, and Aunt Tricia had the day off. Lucy was planning to go in right before the lunch rush started to help Betsy at the counter.

Aunt Tricia buttered a scone and flipped through her customary paper, while Gigi batted at Lucy's leg for a treat. Lucy was just about to give in and go to Gigi's snack cabinet when Aunt Tricia spoke up.

"Well, for Pete's sake!" She frowned and rattled the paper. "That obnoxious man has done it again."

Lucy looked up, startled. "Who?"

"Bob Billings," Aunt Tricia replied crossly, scanning the paper. She harumphed and set the newspaper down on the table, pointing. "Now he's plastered his nonsense as an op-ed in The Ivy Creek Ledger. I would imagine it's because they wouldn't print this rubbish as news."

Lucy peered at the page, seeing the headline:

Solved or Unsolved? The Ivy Creek Murders

Lucy frowned, scanning the op-ed. Billings touted his theory that Ivy Creek had far too many murders in a short amount of time for it to be a random circumstance. Instead, he suggested, perhaps there was a serial killer in their midst, and the citizens were being misled by the authorities. From there, his reasoning got muddy, with vague references to cases in the last year, which Billings claimed had "insufficient evidence" to have actually led to the successful capture and prosecution of the murderers. He wrapped up his ramble by hinting at a coverup.

Lucy sighed. *How ridiculous.* Mr. Billings had purposely left out the fact that in almost all of these cases, the killers, themselves, had signed confessions.

She narrowed her eyes at the final, ominous sentence.

"With the recent murder at The Haunted Forest, we must wonder if this case, too, will be deemed 'solved' quickly by the authorities, and tucked away, out of sight... potentially leaving a serial killer wandering in our midst."

20

"There's not really anything I can do, Lucy," Taylor's voice on the phone sounded grim. "It's an op-ed. I'm surprised that The Ivy Creek Ledger would print a conspiracy theory, but Mr. Billings didn't break any laws."

Lucy huffed out a breath, frustrated. "He's trying to create a panic!"

Taylor was silent for a moment. His tone was gentle when he spoke next. "I'm worried about you, Lucy. You're getting too involved in this case, and you're letting this man get under your skin. You need to just step back and go on with your usual business. Don't worry about Bob Billings."

Lucy mulled over his words. "You're right, Taylor. I shouldn't pay any attention to Mr. Billings. But I can't help but be concerned about the case. Joseph is a very good friend of mine, and Derek is still under suspicion... isn't he?"

The silence stretched between them for a moment, and when Taylor answered, his voice was gruff. "Although Derek's not been ruled out as a suspect, I can tell you he's no longer at the top of my list."

Lucy's mood lightened at his words. "Really? That's great! How about Russ Leighton?"

Taylor gave a dry chuckle. "This is exactly what I mean, Lucy. You need to let me worry about the case. We're making progress, I promise you."

Lucy tamped down the questions springing to her lips. She couldn't help but be curious, but it appeared that Taylor wasn't willing to share the details of the investigation. She took a deep breath, changing the subject.

"I picked up a couple of pumpkins yesterday, at Nelson's Farm."

Taylor responded with such cheer in his voice that Lucy knew he was relieved she'd dropped the subject of the case. "That's great! Shall we carve them together, like usual?"

Lucy was surprised. "Can you make time for that? I know you're busy…"

Taylor assured her, "Of course! It's just one evening. How about tomorrow night?"

Lucy grinned. "Sounds great! Why don't you come for dinner, and we'll carve the pumpkins afterward?"

"Sounds like a plan. Around six-thirty?" he asked.

Lucy agreed and hung up with a smile. It would be nice to spend a little time with Taylor. They hadn't had a date night since The Haunted Forest… and that had turned into a murder investigation!

She hummed to herself as she got dressed for work, pleased to have something to look forward to.

Lucy and Betsy handled the lunch crowd with ease, and by two o'clock, Lucy decided to help Hannah in the kitchen. Today was pie day, and the racks were filled with apple, cherry, and peach pies, fragrant and steaming from the oven.

Betsy poked her head through the archway. "Mrs. Connelly said to tell you guys the spooky house is amazing, and she's going to bring her kids after dark to see it through the window."

"Cool!" Hannah grinned, up to her elbows in dough.

Lucy smiled, reminding herself to change the house's interior light settings to play spooky noises, as well, before she left. "Great! Please tell her thank you, Betsy."

Hannah rolled out some dough and proceeded to cut rounds for turnovers. "I think I'm going to pick up a couple of pumpkins after work."

Lucy laughed. "I just did yesterday, and here I thought I was late!"

Hannah shook her head, amused. "I have this idea for a Halloween card, if I can get Spooky to cooperate. I thought I'd rake some fall leaves into a pile, position the pumpkins, and then try to get Spooky to sit there with them while I take a picture."

Lucy snickered. "Good luck with that. In case you haven't noticed, cats don't exactly obey commands."

Hannah chuckled. "Yes, I've noticed that. So, maybe she won't sit. But I thought if I put some of her favorite treats in the leaves, at least she'd stay right there, then maybe I'll be able to get her to look up for the picture."

Lucy nodded as she scooped fruit filling onto Hannah's rounds of dough. "That actually might work... with a lot of patience!"

Hannah brushed egg wash along the edges before folding the dough over the filling. "Fortunately, I have plenty of patience, and plenty of cat treats. I just need one good shot."

She looked up at Lucy. "Are you and Taylor going to carve jack-o'-lanterns, after all? I figured he was too involved with the case."

Lucy hesitated, wanting to vent about the op-ed, but she realized Taylor was right–she needed to let it go. She simply answered, "Yes! He has a free evening tomorrow," and left it at that.

The rest of the afternoon passed quickly, and Lucy let Hannah go early, finishing up the baking on her own. She admired the changing leaves as she drove home, crimson and gold against the cerulean blue sky. Soon, she was unlocking her front door, greeted by Gigi.

"Where's Aunt Tricia?" she asked the kitty, but Gigi chose not to answer, instead leading Lucy on a winding path to the treat cabinet.

Lucy obliged, shaking two chicken-flavored treats onto the floor before stepping over to the kitchen table. Aunt Tricia had left a note, saying she was running errands, and to call if there was anything they needed at the market.

Lucy opened the freezer, eyeing the pork chops with thoughts of tomorrow's dinner date. She tapped her lip thoughtfully, turning to the pantry. Taylor was enamored of both sweets and apples... maybe some baked apples would make a nice side dish, alongside scalloped potatoes, and pork chops.

She rummaged through the refrigerator, checking her supplies and decided to have Aunt Tricia pick up some cream for the potatoes. The phone rang as she straightened up and Lucy grinned.

"Aunt Tricia is a mind reader," she told Gigi, who regarded her solemnly.

"Hi," Lucy said into the receiver, fully expecting her aunt on the line. She was unprepared for the familiar voice, choking on a sob.

It was Hannah.

"Spooky is missing!" she managed to say, before giving in to tears.

21

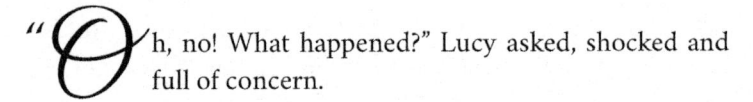

"Oh, no! What happened?" Lucy asked, shocked and full of concern.

Hannah took a deep breath, but her voice shook. "I was out in the yard, trying to take that Halloween picture. You know, I've been keeping Spooky in since I adopted her."

"Right," Lucy said, her heart breaking for her friend.

Hannah said, "She was doing OK, kind of wide-eyed, but not scared, and she seemed to be enjoying the leaves." Her voice trembled. "I put treats down, and she was so cute, scavenging in the leaves to find them."

Hannah sighed; her voice filled with regret. "I wish I'd never brought her outside. A car backfired, and it scared her. The next thing I knew, she bolted, running across the yard." She gulped audibly. "She just disappeared..." Her voice trailed off and Lucy knew her friend had given into tears again.

"I'll be right there," she told Hannah. "We'll look for her together."

In ten minutes, Lucy was at Hannah's place. She could spot her friend in the backyard, looking up into the trees and calling Spooky's name. Lucy approached her, giving her a hug.

Hannah's face was pale, and tear streaked, as she drew back. "Oh, Lucy, what if she can't find her way home? What if she becomes homeless again, and it's all my fault?"

Lucy patted her back, trying to calm her. "We'll find her, Hannah. We'll search high and low, and we can ask your neighbors to keep an eye out, too."

They decided to split up to cover more ground. Lucy spent the next hour walking through the neighborhood, calling Spooky's name, and knocking on doors. She even questioned a group of children playing nearby, asking if they'd seen a black cat with green eyes.

There was no sign of Spooky, and the sun had set a half hour ago. Soon it would be full dark.

Hannah was inconsolable. Lucy hated to leave her friend in that state, but there was nothing else that could be done today.

"I'm OK," Hannah assured Lucy, though her eyes streamed with tears. "You need to go home. I'm going to make up some flyers to post with her picture on them."

Lucy thought that was a good idea. "Why don't you take tomorrow off to look for her? We got a lot done today at the bakery."

Hannah looked grateful. "Thank you, Lucy. Maybe I'll find her in the morning. Or, you never know, she might come back tonight when she gets hungry." Her voice held a note of hope. "I'm going to leave the windows open, so I'll hear her if she meows."

Lucy hugged her friend goodbye. "She'll come back, Hannah. Don't fret."

THE NEXT DAY, Lucy called to check on Hannah, and was saddened to hear that Spooky had not reappeared. The heartbreak in her friend's voice went straight through Lucy, as she could well imagine how she'd feel if something ever happened to Gigi. There was not much she could do, however, except be supportive and pray that Hannah would find her little cat.

She tried to tuck the sadness away as she prepared Taylor's favorite foods that evening, chatting with Aunt Tricia as she cooked.

"What are you going to do with the spooky house after Halloween?" Aunt Tricia asked.

In previous years Lucy had raffled the seasonal decoration off, but she'd been too preoccupied this year with the murder at The Haunted Forest.

Lucy checked the gravy simmering on the stove, and adjusted the heat. "There's an orphanage in Colby. I think it would be a welcome treat for the kids if I donated it there."

Aunt Tricia nodded approvingly. "Those kids don't get a lot of nice surprises in their lives. I think that's a splendid idea."

Lucy opened the oven door and withdrew the pork chops, covering them with foil, and checked the baked apples and scalloped potatoes. A few more minutes, and everything would be ready. She felt a buzz of excitement in her heart at seeing Taylor again, in a date night setting. They were both usually so busy. These times together, away from either of their jobs, were few and far between.

She imagined his reaction to her home cooked meal and smiled. Above all else, Lucy got immense satisfaction from feeding good food to people she cared about.

"Another helping, Taylor?" Aunt Tricia asked, offering the chafing dish of scalloped potatoes.

Taylor grinned, holding his sides, and shook his head. "I couldn't possibly eat another bite." He looked at Lucy, his expression tender. "That was the best meal I've had in a long time, Lucy. Thank you."

Lucy blushed and looked away, pleased at the compliment.

Aunt Tricia rose from the table, announcing she was going to make some coffee.

"Any news on Spooky?" Taylor asked. Lucy had called him that afternoon, asking him to spread the word.

She shook her head sadly. "Not yet. Poor Hannah."

Taylor patted her hand consolingly. "I'm sure she'll find her."

Together, they cleared the dishes and brought them into the kitchen, the scent of coffee riding the air. Aunt Tricia insisted on loading the dishwasher herself, shooing the two of them outside.

"Go on, now, or you'll lose the light before you carve the pumpkins."

Lucy and Taylor stepped out onto the porch, where Lucy had laid out their carving tools next to the pumpkins, along with a sheaf of newspapers. After a few minutes of relaxing with their coffee in twin rockers, they decided to get down to business.

Lucy carefully marked out a symmetrical smiling face on her pumpkin with a sharpie marker, laughing when she glanced over at Taylor's handiwork. He'd drawn a menacing face; eyes tilted evilly, with jagged brows, and a lopsided toothy grin.

"Your pumpkin is scaring my pumpkin," she joked, as they both began to carefully cut out circles around the stems.

"That's the whole point of Halloween," he countered with a grin.

Within minutes, the caps were ready to be lifted away. Lucy peered down at the innards of her pumpkin, wrinkling her nose. "This is my least favorite part," she said. "It's so slimy!"

Taylor stopped, his hand halfway into his own pumpkin. "Do you want me to scoop out the seeds for you?"

Lucy chuckled at his chivalry, shaking her head. "No, I have latex gloves." She donned the pair she'd stashed on the porch.

"Oh, *now* you tell me you have gloves," Taylor teased, and Lucy laughed, feeling the tension of the past week evaporate as she and Taylor focused on creating the perfect jack-o'-lanterns.

Fifteen minutes later, the pumpkins were scraped clean, and Lucy popped battery operated lights inside while Taylor disposed of the trash. He returned and stood arm in arm with Lucy on the walkway, gazing at their creations in the gathering dusk.

Taylor's menacing jack-o'-lantern glowed alongside Lucy's happy faced one, and she smiled at the sight, enjoying the crisp October air on her skin, and the warmth of Taylor's arm looped around her waist.

If only all of their memories of this Halloween could have been so pleasant.

22

Two days passed, and Spooky was still missing. Hannah was inconsolable, her face drawn and pale as she worked, her usual sparkling personality buried beneath worry and self-recrimination. Lucy was as supportive as she could be, putting up additional flyers around town and even inside the bakery itself. The more time that passed, however, the less likely it seemed that Spooky would return.

Equally as worrisome, was the alarm that was beginning to take hold of Ivy Creek's citizens in the wake of Bob Billings' op ed. Whispers were heard regarding the possible police cover-up, and the townspeople became jumpy and argumentative, as confidence in their police department began to wane. *Was there a serial killer among them?* Opinion was beginning to shift in that direction.

Betsy was polishing the glass of the pastry counter during an afternoon lull, while Lucy erased the morning's specials from the chalkboard.

"I overheard Brenda Mills this morning saying a lot of parents won't be letting their kids go trick or treating Halloween night."

Lucy looked over at her, surprised. "Not at all? I think as long as they were closely supervised or driven from house to house, it would be OK. Taylor said he'll have plenty of officers patrolling the streets to make it safe."

Betsy shook her head. "She said people are so jumpy, thinking one of Ivy Creek's residents is a serial killer. They don't even trust their neighbors anymore. They're afraid the candy might be poisoned."

Lucy frowned, setting down her eraser. *Bob Billings had done so much damage to the morale of Ivy Creek.* It just wasn't right.

She turned, hearing Aunt Tricia's steps descending the staircase. The older woman had taken advantage of the couch in Lucy's office to take a break.

"Feeling any better?" she asked her aunt, concerned at the weariness on the older woman's face.

Aunt Tricia smiled wanly and shook her head, admitting, "This is my own fault. What with all the tension in town these days, and trying to read Dracula with the book club, I'm not getting any decent sleep. The little bit I do manage to get is full of haunted castles and blood sucking demons." She chuckled dryly.

Lucy asked, "Aren't you meeting with the book club tonight?"

Her aunt nodded, pouring herself a cup of coffee. "Yes, we're meeting at Sandy Peloza's, right down the street from our house."

Lucy was relieved her aunt wouldn't be driving after dark, as tired as she seemed. "Maybe you should feel out the other members... it's possible some others are feeling too anxious right now to be reading horror, the same as you. Is it really too late to start a new book?"

Aunt Tricia stirred sugar and cream into her cup. "We are a good part of the way through this one, but you're right. Lucy. I may not be the only one having sleepless nights. I'll bring it up at the meeting tonight."

The door to the kitchen swung open and Hannah emerged, bearing a tray of oatmeal raisin cookies. She was uncharacteristically silent as she replenished the tray inside the pastry case, and all three women regarded her sympathetically.

Hannah glanced up, her blue eyes swollen from recent tears. "That's the rest of the cookies for today. Anything else we're low on?"

Lucy shook her head, and Hannah asked, "Do you mind if I go home a little early, then? I was thinking of checking back in at some houses near me to see if anyone's seen Spooky."

Lucy said, "Sure, of course, Hannah. I'll see you in the morning."

"Good luck," called Betsy, and Aunt Tricia added her well wishes, too.

"The poor dear," Aunt Tricia murmured after they heard the back door shut a minute later, indicating Hannah had gone.

"I know." Lucy looked troubled. "I wish I could do more to help."

The front bell jangled, and the women looked up to see Derek enter the bakery.

"Well, this is a nice surprise!" Betsy greeted him with a grin on her face.

Lucy and Aunt Tricia smiled at the young man, saying hello. Lucy noticed Derek, too, had shadows of unhappiness on his face.

"How are you, Derek?" asked Betsy, her brows furrowed. She had noticed the same thing.

Derek sighed. "Alright, I guess. I figured I'd stop by and tell you this myself. I've already told Joseph and he's not happy with me."

Betsy looked alarmed. "What's happened? Is it the…" she trailed off, afraid to bring up the police's interest in him as a suspect.

Derek's gaze lingered on the fresh oatmeal raisin cookies, and Lucy slipped one out of the case, wrapped in deli paper, and handed it over the counter. He accepted it with a grateful look.

"It's not the murder case, don't worry," he reassured Betsy, taking a bite. He closed his eyes briefly, enjoying the treat, before continuing.

"I'm going to drop out of school," he announced, and all three women looked at him in shock.

"But… why?" Betsy asked, dismay on her face.

Derek shrugged. "it's not the same anymore. I'm a theater major, and I feel like I can't be active in the theater community right now. I mean, my friends don't suspect me, but I can't try out for anything at Ivy Creek's Playhouse right now, for obvious reasons. It seems like I'm spinning my wheels, just taking classes, but not really acting."

Lucy jumped in. "You need to look at the big picture, Derek. The case will get solved, and you'll be exonerated. Then you can get back into the swing." Her brow wrinkled. *The decisions Derek made right now would affect his career. He had to see that.*

Derek chewed thoughtfully, but then he shrugged again, swallowing. "All I know is it doesn't feel right anymore. It feels like I'm wasting my time."

"What did Joseph say?" asked Aunt Tricia, and the young man gave a wry smile.

"Pretty much what Lucy just said. Look at the big picture. Don't get caught up in the moment." He looked around at the three of them and sighed.

"Well, I'll think about it for a few more days, I guess." He looked at his watch. "I should go. I'm meeting a friend on campus."

He said his goodbyes, and the three ladies watched him walk out of the bakery into the late afternoon sun.

"Oh, boy," Betsy shook her head. "I bet Joseph is not pleased about this."

"It would be a shame for that boy to give up on his dream because of this mess," Aunt Tricia said, and Lucy murmured her agreement.

If only the police would catch a break in the case before it was too late.

LUCY LAY on the couch under her favorite throw blanket, channel surfing with Gigi settled beside her. Aunt Tricia should be home any minute, she thought, watching the gathering gloom nervously. They lived on a quiet street where they knew all their neighbors, but considering recent events… Lucy pushed that thought out of her head, deciding she'd wait another ten minutes before she'd allow herself to worry.

Five minutes later, footsteps were heard on the front porch, and Lucy sat up, watching as the door swung open.

Aunt Tricia stepped inside quickly, and slammed the door shut behind her, bolting it and immediately looking through the peephole. She turned back around and leaned against the door, her breath coming in gasps.

"Auntie?" Lucy asked, alarmed by the woman's actions. "What is it?"

Aunt Tricia started putting a hand to her chest, apparently not having noticed Lucy on the couch.

"Oh, my," she gasped, taking a moment to catch her breath. "I didn't see you!"

She straightened up and turned, peering through the peephole once more.

"Auntie, what happened?" Lucy asked, rising from the couch. She was growing more worried by the second.

Aunt Tricia turned back to look at Lucy, her eyes wide and full of fear.

"Someone was following me!"

23

"Followed?" echoed Lucy. "Are you sure?"

She approached the door, peering through the peephole, herself. She could see nothing amiss, just the front stoop illuminated by the porch light.

"I am absolutely certain," stated Aunt Tricia. "I had only just left Sandy's house when I heard footsteps behind me. I turned around and saw a man, but he was a little way back, so I thought nothing of it... until..." Her voice was tremulous, and Lucy guided her over to a chair to sit.

"What happened then?" Lucy prompted. As upset as Aunt Tricia was, she couldn't help but wonder if the woman's imagination had run away with her. Her aunt had been very jumpy as of late, and not well rested.

Aunt Tricia laid a hand at the base of her throat, closing her eyes briefly. "I heard the footsteps quicken, like he was trying to catch up to me, so I turned around again."

Her eyes popped open, wide and full of fear. "I saw the same man duck behind a light post, like he didn't want to be seen! That's when I started to panic. I kept walking, faster and faster, and I could hear him doing the same, but when I dared to look back, he must have hidden again. But I know he was there!"

Lucy frowned. That certainly was suspicious behavior. "Did you see what he looked like?"

Aunt Tricia shook her head. "All I can say for sure is, it was a man wearing a long black coat with a hood."

Lucy stiffened in alarm. *A long, black coat with a hood?*

"I'm calling Taylor, right now," she said, grabbing her phone from the coffee table.

Taylor picked up on the second ring, and Lucy quickly filled him in on what had happened.

"I'll be right there," he told her. "There's a unit in your area, so they may arrive first. Keep your doors locked." His tone was urgent as he imparted the warning, and Lucy shivered.

Had Aunt Tricia just encountered the killer?

Minutes later, there was a knock on the door, and a voice identified the visitor as the Ivy Creek Police. Taking no chances, Lucy looked through the peephole before allowing them entry. One of the officers came in to take a statement from Aunt Tricia, while the other canvassed the street.

Taylor arrived a few minutes later. By then, Aunt Tricia was feeling more herself, slightly rattled, but calm enough to offer him a cup of tea. While she was in the kitchen, Taylor drew Lucy aside.

"I'd like to keep the story that Russ told quiet," he said. "Particularly the detail of the long, black coat with the hood. Did you mention it to your aunt?"

Lucy shook her head. "No, and that's why I'm worried! Taylor, do you think it was him? The same man who killed Tony Newton? Is he targeting Aunt Tricia?" She kept her voice low, but her tone was near panic.

Taylor took her hands. "Lucy, we don't know anything for sure. But I want you to promise me that neither of you will go outside alone at night. Keep your doors and windows locked. I'll have a unit patrolling your street."

Lucy met his eyes and nodded. "I promise."

Taylor squeezed her hands and released her. "OK. I'll come by the bakery tomorrow and let you know if we've found anything."

Lucy nodded, suddenly feeling weary as the adrenaline faded.

She wished this whole nightmare was over with.

Lucy yawned as she finished piping chocolate ganache on the eclairs. Last night's excitement had taken its toll, and as weary as she'd felt, her anxiety had kept her awake.

She'd told Aunt Tricia at breakfast that Taylor wanted to keep the incident quiet while the police investigated, and her aunt agreed not to share her experience. Lucy paused her work briefly, wondering how Aunt Tricia was faring out front. The poor dear had barely got any rest herself last night.

The phone rang and Betsy appeared in the archway.

"Hannah! It's for you."

Hannah accepted the receiver and said hello. Suddenly, she stood stock upright, her eyes wide. Concerned, Lucy crossed the room to stand at her side.

"Yes! Oh, thank God, you found her! Yes, I can come right away. Hold on, let me get a pen," Hannah looked around frantically, and Lucy quickly found a notepad and pen, passing it to her.

Hannah scribbled an address, and ripped the sheet from the pad, saying, "No, I'm not familiar with it, but I have a GPS. I'll be there as soon as I can. I'm leaving right away! Thank you so much!"

Lucy looked at Hannah, barely daring to hope as her friend hung up the phone.

"Is it…?" Lucy ventured, almost afraid to say it, but Hannah nodded eagerly, her eyes shining with happiness.

"Someone found Spooky! I need to go get her right now." Suddenly, she winced. "Oh, gosh, I forgot. I rode my bike in to work. Lucy, can I take your car?"

Lucy nodded immediately. "Of course you can! Where was she found?"

Hannah consulted the paper. "473 Gibbons Avenue. Do you know where that is? The fellow said it's on the outskirts of town, but I don't recognize the street."

Lucy shook her head, feeling a sudden prickle of unease. "No, but I'll go with you. We'll just punch it into the GPS." She'd feel better if Hannah didn't go to meet a stranger alone, especially after what had occurred last night.

Hannah looked grateful. "Thanks, Lucy! I'm so excited I'd probably drive right past the house and not see it!" She closed her eyes, sighing with relief. "Thank goodness, my Spooky is coming home!"

Lucy smiled, so happy for her friend. They turned off the ovens and updated Aunt Tricia and Betsy on what had happened. Within two minutes, they were climbing into Lucy's SUV, where Hannah read out the address while Lucy punched it into the GPS.

Then they were off, heading west out of Ivy Creek proper. They drove for about ten minutes before the GPS turned them onto an unfamiliar road. Another turn and they were in an area that held a lot of abandoned houses, some for sale, and others in a state of disrepair.

"Wow, poor Spooky," Hannah commented, looking out the window. "The poor girl really got turned around, to make it all the way out here."

Lucy tried not to worry as they drove further into the neglected neighborhoods. They turned onto Gibbons Ave, but most of the houses left standing didn't have numbers visible.

"How much further does the GPS say?" she asked Hannah, keeping her eyes on the road.

Hannah consulted the device and replied, "It should be coming up on the right in a minute."

The GPS suddenly announced, "You have arrived."

Lucy slowed to a stop, peering at the old house before them. The paint was peeling, and two of the windows had cracked panes. The yard was full of weeds and debris.

"Is this it?" she asked, her voice uncertain. The house looked abandoned.

Hannah scanned the property for a number. "Yes! Look, there's the number!" The brass numbers were hung near the door, with the number three hanging crookedly.

Lucy frowned. "I don't know, Hannah. This doesn't look right. That house looks abandoned."

Hannah was already exiting the car. "The guy said he was renovating an old house."

Lucy had no choice but to follow her friend, though she wished Hannah had agreed to meet somewhere in public.

"Well, where's his vehicle?" she countered, but Hannah just shrugged and continued up the walkway.

They climbed the steps and paused in front of the door. As far as Lucy could tell, there were no lights on inside. She was starting to feel very uneasy.

Maybe they should call Taylor.

"Hannah, wait," she requested, but Hannah had already raised a hand to knock. As her knuckles made contact with the door, it swung inward, revealing a dark interior.

"Hello?" called Hannah, stepping into the gloom.

24

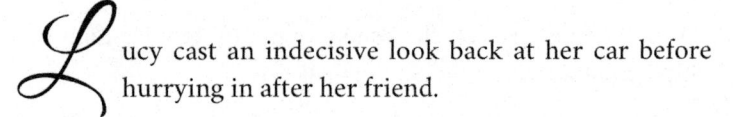

Lucy cast an indecisive look back at her car before hurrying in after her friend.

"Hannah!" she hissed. "Wait!"

But Hannah was striding forward into the front room, calling out, "Hello! It's Hannah Curry! I've come to pick up Spooky." She disappeared through the archway at the end of the room, presumedly into a hallway.

Hannah's voice echoed back to her, and Lucy looked around nervously, seeing the few pieces of furniture in the parlor were covered with sheets. There were leaves and debris scattered on the floor, apparently blown in through the fireplace. The place smelled musty, unused. Lucy was certain no one was living here.

"Hannah?" she called. "I want to call Taylor." She took a few more steps forward, but Hannah didn't answer.

"Hannah?"

Lucy stopped where she was, listening, but was met with absolute silence. Her heart began to pound as she slowly approached the archway that Hannah had gone through.

"Hannah?" she whispered, and turned the corner, peering into the dark hallway. She blinked and her eyes adjusted to the gloom. Her breath caught.

There was a form lying on the floor at the end of the hallway!

Lucy rushed over; her worst fears confirmed. It was Hannah, and she was unconscious.

"Hannah, Hannah," Lucy said frantically, patting her friend's cheeks. Hannah was breathing, but out cold. Lucy couldn't see any injuries. She reached for her phone to dial 911.

A noise from behind her had her turning around, but before she could see what it was, Lucy was grabbed roughly in a headlock. A cold, damp cloth was pressed firmly over her nose and mouth.

Chloroform... was her final, horrified thought, before everything went black.

Lucy's mind was fuzzy, and she had a terrible headache. She opened her eyes, confused by her surroundings, as her eyes struggled to focus. Shadows and light swam in and out of her vision, and a dark figure was standing before her.

Where was she?

"Ah, so you've decided to join us." The words were spoken with such underlying malice that Lucy jerked backward, making her head pound even more. She recognized that voice.

She blinked rapidly, and the man came into focus.

It was Bob Billings. He was wearing a long, black coat with the hood folded down. His dark eyes gleamed behind his spectacles.

"Surprised?" he asked smugly, watching for her reaction.

Suddenly, it all came rushing back.

Hannah!

Lucy whipped her head from side to side and saw Hannah slumped in a chair a few feet away, bound and gagged. She was apparently still unconscious.

Lucy struggled to rise, finding she, too, was tied to a chair with her arms behind her. Her voice was muffled through the gag as she shouted for help, and she knew no one would hear her. She glared at the man in front of her.

He smirked. "Oh, Lucy Hale… you thought you were so smart, didn't you? All your amateur detective work, trying to find that boy's killer. But you never thought of me, did you?"

He laughed and Lucy suppressed a shudder at the sound, so gleeful and malevolent.

"Well, I imagine you have questions." He fiddled with an object, lost in thought, and Lucy glanced down, her eyes widening in horror.

He wore black gloves. In his hands was a length of dirty clothesline, no doubt scavenged from the debris on the floor.

He was going to kill them.

25

The reporter's face twisted into a cruel smile as he tracked Lucy's gaze to the rope in his hands. With a sudden move, he snapped the length between his hands, and it made an ominous pop. Lucy flinched, and Billings laughed.

"Not to worry, Ms. Hale. At least, not for the moment." He sneered, looking over at Hannah, who was still out cold. "I'll be waiting until your friend wakes up before the real fun begins. Killing someone who can't struggle would take all the fun out of it." He smiled sadistically, a dark joy upon his face.

Lucy felt sick with dread. The man was clearly mad.

She looked around, seeing they were in the front parlor of the abandoned house. She closed her eyes briefly, her mind scrambling for a solution.

Were any of the neighboring houses occupied? With a sinking feeling, she was suddenly certain they were not. Obviously, the man had chosen this remote location so no one would hear or see anything. Behind her chair, Lucy's numbed fingers explored the knots, trying to find a way to get loose.

Her captor began to pace the room. "You're probably wondering why, aren't you?" He fixed her with a hard look. "Part of this is your fault, you know. You were one of the many people in Ivy Creek who thought I could be dismissed. Flicked away, like an ant."

His anger seemed to build as he resumed pacing, kicking debris out of his path. "I thought I could make a new start in Ivy Creek... find fame as a star reporter. I even dreamed *Bob Billings* would be a household name some day!" He whirled around to glare at her, and Lucy's hands stilled, afraid he'd see what she was doing.

"I'm an excellent journalist!" He insisted, as though Lucy had argued with him. His face was full of rage. "But no one here would give me a chance."

His hands were fisted tightly around the rope. Suddenly, he sighed, his shoulders drooping, before continuing his pacing, pensively now.

"It was supposed to be just the one murder. That was my original plan. I thought by killing that Newton boy at The Haunted Forest, and writing an exclusive, behind the scenes article about it... I truly believed that would be enough. I thought doors would open for me."

He frowned with displeasure. "But the only paper that would print my story was The Ivy Creek Voice." He barked out a harsh laugh, turning to Lucy once more.

"And then they wouldn't even print my second article about a serial killer in Ivy Creek! That... rag... refused me, saying my story wasn't in the town's best interest. To get it printed at all, I had to resort to submitting it as an op-ed." He shook his head in disgust. "An op-ed, like an amateur!"

He suddenly flexed the length of rope between his hands, stepping closer to Lucy. She drew back, her eyes wide as he spat out his words, fury in his eyes.

"Now I have no choice! To avoid ridicule, I *must* create an actual serial killer in Ivy Creek. No one will doubt my theory after your bodies are found, so soon after the first murder. And once I write a series of articles - *exclusive articles* - about the Ivy Creek murders, everyone will finally recognize my talent!" He paused, his eyes thoughtful, and added conversationally, "I believe I'll write a book about it, as well. Who knows? They might even offer me a movie deal."

His expression lightened, becoming eager at the notion. He approached Hannah, and Lucy's chest tightened, praying he wouldn't hurt her friend.

"It's time," he snapped out, patting Hannah's cheeks impatiently. "Wake up, princess."

Hannah started to stir, and Lucy began to tremble uncontrollably. She feared as soon as Hannah was fully awake, the man would murder them both. Lucy shouted through her gag, trying to distract him.

Suddenly, the sound of a window breaking at the back of the house startled them all.

Bob Billings froze, his attention focused on the hallway. He took a few hesitant steps in that direction, pressing himself against the far wall to peer through the archway.

The front door exploded inward, and Taylor came barreling through, rushing past Lucy so quickly he was almost a blur. He tackled Bob Billings from behind, bringing him down with a hard thud, just as another officer appeared from the back of the house, blocking the hallway.

Taylor pressed the reporter's face to the floor, his knee upon the man's back, while Billings' muffled voice could be heard whining about police brutality.

Taylor looked at Lucy, his face lined with worry, as he cuffed the man.

"Are you OK?"

She nodded; grateful tears rolling down her cheeks.

Taylor relinquished Billings to the other officer, who began to read the man his rights, and Taylor knelt quickly behind Lucy, cutting her bindings and removing her gag. He took her into his arms, holding her close as she shuddered.

Lucy whispered, "Hannah?" against his shoulder, her voice clogged with tears.

Setting Lucy gently back down in the chair, Taylor pulled out his radio, calling for an ambulance, and hurried over to Hannah.

She was now fully awake, but she seemed confused as Taylor released her and pulled off her gag.

She met Lucy's eyes. "What happened?" She looked around at the ramshackle room, clearly distressed. "Where's Spooky?"

Lucy's heart sank, fearing that Bob Billings had killed Hannah's pet. But Taylor spoke up, crouching in front of Hannah and reassuring her.

"Spooky's safe and sound, at the bakery," he said in a calming tone. "She was never here. Betsy found her out by the dumpster, shortly after you left, and called me, afraid you had been tricked."

Hannah blinked away tears, her eyes locked on his face. "She's safe? She came home?"

Taylor nodded, confirming in a gentle tone, "Yes. She came home to you, Hannah."

Lucy smiled through her tears as Hannah cried out her joy, her hands clutching Taylor's sleeve.

26

"Well, this will certainly be a Halloween to remember," Taylor remarked, accepting the mug of hot cider that Joseph passed over to him, and nodding his thanks.

"Personally, I'd rather forget it," Lucy remarked, but grinned up at him.

They were all sitting at the large patio table in Lucy's backyard, two days after the horrific encounter with Bob Billings. Aunt Tricia and Betsy were in the kitchen, plating up cinnamon-pecan coffee cake, and Hannah was on her way.

The beautiful autumn afternoon seemed the perfect time to gather together and celebrate that Lucy and Hannah had been unharmed, thanks to Taylor's quick thinking and heroic actions.

The back door opened, and Betsy and Aunt Tricia came out, passing out napkins and plates of cake.

"Where's Hannah?" Betsy asked, taking a seat at Joseph's side. "I thought she would be here by now."

Lucy was about to answer, when suddenly they heard a car door shut out front. A minute later, Hannah appeared, carrying a blue cat carrier, with Spooky peering out through the metal grates, her green eyes luminous. She meowed as she saw her favorite people gathered.

"Hello!" Hannah called out, letting herself in the back gate and securing it behind herself. She approached the table, setting the carrier down on the ground. "Spooky was microchipped this morning, and I didn't want to leave her alone." She glanced around the yard, which was enclosed by a tall privacy fence.

"If it's OK with you, Lucy, I think I'll let her out."

Lucy nodded, watching with a smile as Hannah opened the door of the carrier. Spooky poked her face out timidly, looking around at the new surroundings, while Hannah joined them at the table, pulling up a chair.

"Momma's right here, baby," Hannah crooned, keeping an eye on the cat. "You're OK."

Encouraged, Spooky crept out of the carrier and sidled over to the flower garden, sniffing delicately. Within minutes, she'd found some tasty greens to chew.

"How are you feeling, Hannah?" Betsy asked, passing her a slice of cake. Joseph poured her a mug of cider from the carafe.

"Oh, yum," Hannah took a bite and a sip before answering. "I'm good. The headache's gone, finally. And it's so great to have Spooky back home!"

Both Hannah and Lucy had been brought from the abandoned house directly to the hospital to be checked out, and both were released later that evening. Although Lucy bounced back right away, the chloroform had affected Hannah differently, plaguing her with a lingering headache.

Hannah turned to Taylor, a puzzled look on her face. "I'm sure Lucy already knows, but you never did tell me, Taylor. How in the world did you find us at that abandoned house?"

Taylor chuckled, but before he could answer, Betsy jumped in. "It was the coolest thing!"

Her eyes sparkled, and she glanced at Taylor with admiration. "When none of us could reach you guys on the phone, Taylor asked for the notepad you'd written the address on. He did this thing with a pencil, shading over the impression left on the notepad… and voila! He had the address!"

Hannah raised her eyebrows, impressed. "Wow. That's some trick!"

Lucy squeezed Taylor's arm affectionately. "He's a good man to have around," she said, and Taylor smiled down at her, his blue eyes warm.

"Indeed," Aunt Tricia agreed, nodding her head. She smiled at Hannah. "So glad you're feeling better, dear, and that you've got your furry baby home."

"Cheers to that!" Joseph said, raising his cider for a toast. Stoneware clinked as they all joined him, a chorus of voices around the table.

"Cheers!"

Lucy sipped her cider and turned to Taylor. "Any word on the trial date for Bob Billings?"

Taylor swallowed his last bite of cake, brushing crumbs from his fingers. "Not yet. He'll be arraigned on Monday. I can't imagine there will be any problems convicting him. The man is such a braggart that he confessed it all on tape. He even requested a copy of his booking photo, wanting to include it in a future book. Can you imagine?"

"Future book?" Betsy looked aghast. "He's going to write a book from prison? As a convicted killer?"

Taylor nodded; his mouth set in a hard line. "Apparently, fame is so important to the man, he'll do whatever it takes to get in the news."

Lucy shook her head, disgusted at the way Billings had so cavalierly taken a young man's life, just to have his own name remembered as a star reporter. Now he'd be remembered as a killer, but it was all the same to him. Fame was fame.

Hannah stated flatly, "He's a madman." She glanced over at Spooky, thankful Bob Billings hadn't really found her pet. "I'm actually glad I was unconscious during all of his crazy rambling. It would have given me nightmares."

Lucy changed the subject to a more pleasant one. "So, Joseph, what's the word on the play? Is The Sword and the Stone still on for next month?"

Joseph beamed, glad to have good news to share. "It is! And, I'm pleased to add, Derek will be playing the lead role now that the case has been solved."

There was applause from around the table, and Spooky looked over curiously at the noise.

Just then, the flap on the cat door opened, and Gigi appeared on the brick walkway, blinking in the sunlight, and looking around herself. It was obvious the moment she saw Spooky, her eyes widening in surprise.

"Uh oh," Hannah whispered to Lucy. "Should I put Spooky in her carrier?"

Lucy watched Gigi, who seemed curious, but not territorial. "No, let's wait and see. I think they'll be fine."

They all watched as Gigi sat where she was, curling her tail primly around her feet, and lifting her face in a haughty pose, choosing to ignore the intruder.

Spooky approached the Persian cautiously, with a soft meow, to which Gigi did not respond. The black feline seemed to be aware it was Gigi's territory, and she laid down a few feet away on the brick, rolling on her back a bit to show her belly.

Lucy smiled. Spooky was acknowledging Gigi was dominant. That was a good start to their friendship. Gigi watched the other cat's antics for a few minutes before turning away, padding over to the cat door with a dignified air, and disappearing inside.

Spooky looked at Hannah and meowed, seeming disappointed, and they all laughed.

The group chatted and enjoyed their refreshments until the daylight began to fade, and the air became cool. Then Betsy, Joseph, Hannah, and Spooky took their leave, with hugs all around.

Taylor helped Lucy and Aunt Tricia clear the dishes, and once they'd finished, Lucy looked up at him, her face soft with tenderness.

"Can you stay awhile?" she asked, and Taylor grinned.

"Yes. My responsibilities have lightened considerably, as of two days ago," he joked, pulling her in for a hug.

They walked around to the front together and lit their jack-o'-lanterns, standing arm in arm in the yard for a moment to appreciate the eerie glow.

"That's about as scary as I want my Halloween to be," Lucy said, nodding at Taylor's menacing jack-o'-lantern. "Fun-scary, not dangerous-scary." She couldn't help but shiver, and Taylor rubbed her arm consolingly.

"C'mon, let's go celebrate Halloween the old-fashioned way," he suggested. "We can eat too much candy and watch a scary movie." Seeing her expression, he amended, "but not too scary!"

Lucy laughed, and led him inside, where Aunt Tricia was relaxing in her favorite chair in the living room.

"Aunt Tricia, do you want to watch a movie with us? I'm going to make some popcorn," Lucy said, plumping the pillows on the couch.

Aunt Tricia smiled, setting her magazine down. "Sounds like fun. What shall we watch?"

Taylor grinned at her with a devilish glint in his eye.

"I was thinking... Dracula!"

The End

SWEET DELIGHTS BAKERY'S CHOCOLATE SUGAR COOKIE DOUGH

1 cup softened butter
12 oz. brown sugar
4 oz. semi-sweet chocolate, melted
2 eggs
1/2 tsp vanilla
3 1/2 cups all-purpose flour
1/2 cup unsweetened cocoa
1 TBL baking powder
2 TBL milk

In a large bowl, beat butter with brown sugar until light and fluffy. Add vanilla extract. Add melted, cooled semi-sweet chocolate, mix well with spatula. Add eggs, one at a time. Mix until well incorporated. Make sure to scrape the sides of the bowl.

Sift together flour, cocoa, and baking powder. Stir into mixture, adding milk as needed, until you have a stiff but malleable dough.

Roll out to ¼" thickness. Cut into desired shapes. Bake on aluminum foil-lined baking sheets in a 350-degree Fahrenheit oven. If using for house construction, bake 10 minutes, trim to template again, then bake another 15 minutes, or until very hard.

*Aluminum foil is used in place of parchment to allow you to add crushed hard candies to window openings, without sticking. If adding candies, crush fine, spoon into window openings of pre-baked pieces after cooling, and bake 5-7 minutes, or until candy is melted. Cool completely before removing from pan

AFTERWORD

Thank you for reading ***Dough Shall Not Murder***. I really hope you enjoyed reading it as much as I had writing it!

If you have a minute, please consider leaving a review on Amazon or the retailer where you got it.

Many thanks in advance for your support!

DEADLY BITES ON WINTER NIGHTS

CHAPTER 1 SNEAK PEEK

CHAPTER 1 SNEAK PEEK

"Did you hear the weather report?" Betsy asked, her eyes merry as she came bustling through the front door of Sweet Delights Bakery. "They say we might get snow this weekend!"

Lucy couldn't help but smile, glancing over from her task of writing specials on the bakery chalkboard. Betsy was her youngest employee, in her early twenties, and her enthusiasm was infectious.

Hannah Curry groaned theatrically, setting down her tray of freshly baked turnovers. As Lucy's star baker, she'd had to prepare double the usual amount of pastries this morning. The chilly December mornings seemed to have whet the appetite of Ivy Creek's citizens.

"Not more snow," Hannah complained, though her lips twitched with humor. "We still have snow on the ground from last week."

Betsy wrinkled her nose as she tied on her apron. "Only an inch or two, and it's dirty."

Aunt Tricia added her two cents, not looking up as she stocked the cash register for the day. "It would be nice to have a fresh blanket of snow on the ground for Christmas." She finished and turned to regard Lucy. "When are you and Taylor planning to go get the tree for our house?"

Taylor Baker was Ivy Creek's deputy sheriff, and Lucy's beau. He was a frequent dinner guest at Lucy and Aunt Tricia's house; the home that Lucy had grown up in. Lucy's parents had tragically passed away less than two years ago, prompting Lucy to move back from the city where she'd worked as a food blogger. She'd taken over the family's bakery business with some misgivings at first, but now she couldn't imagine doing anything else.

"We were hoping to go one day this week," Lucy answered, carefully printing the new holiday coffee flavors in chalk. "I'm planning to buy a few wreaths as well, one for here and one for the house. Nelson Farm has such a great selection!"

"Oooh, I want to go, too!" Betsy called out. She'd gotten right to work, wiping down the glass top of the pastry case. "And Joseph will, too, of course. We're going to decorate a tree at his house." She sighed happily. "This will be our first Christmas together."

"Count me in, too," added Hannah. "I'm not sure about a tree, because Spooky might climb it. But I need a holiday wreath." Spooky was Hannah's new cat, a stray she had rescued during the Halloween season.

"OK, that sounds like fun!" Lucy grinned. "A group outing. Aunt Tricia, do you want to come with us?"

Aunt Tricia waved a hand. "As much as I like the *look of winter* - through the window of a warm house - I'm not too fond of tromping around outside this time of year. I'll pass, dear."

Lucy nodded understandingly. "OK. I'll talk to Taylor tonight and let you guys know when. Thankfully, things have been pretty calm in town lately, and he's been able to work regular hours."

She suppressed a shudder thinking of last October, when Taylor had worked around the clock to solve the murder at the Haunted Forest attraction, where one of the actors had become a victim. During the investigation, Lucy had unknowingly put herself on the killer's radar, and she and Hannah had barely escaped with their lives.

Hannah surveyed the full pastry case, hands on her hips. "That ought to do it, for the morning rush, anyway," she commented. Turning to Lucy, she asked, "What's next?"

Lucy tapped her chin thoughtfully for a moment. "Fruitcake," she decided. "I dug out Mom's old recipe and made a few tweaks. I think we should start with fifteen cakes and go from there."

Hannah gave a mock salute and headed back into the kitchen. Lucy glanced around the bakery, seeming bare now that they'd taken down the Thanksgiving decorations.

"Betsy," she said, knowing this was a task the young woman would love. "There's a box in the office marked Christmas decorations. Could you run upstairs and grab it, please? I think we should start with hanging the snowflakes."

Betsy face was wreathed in smiles as she nodded, hurrying away. Aunt Tricia poured herself a peppermint mocha and tilted her head, regarding Lucy speculatively.

Lucy raised her eyebrows. She knew that look. Aunt Tricia was scheming.

"What?" she finally asked, unable to guess what was on her aunt's mind.

Aunt Tricia just smiled and shook her head slightly. She sipped her coffee for a moment before she spoke.

"I was just thinking of your parents," she said, nostalgia softening her face. "They got engaged at Christmas, you know."

Lucy nodded. "Yes. I know." She'd heard the story many times.

Aunt Tricia's lips curved. "Christmas is such a nice time to make a lifelong commitment..." She let the words trail off.

Lucy laughed. "Auntie!" She shook her head with amusement and turned away.

Her aunt was always dropping hints that she and Taylor should get married. It was true; they had known each other forever. They'd been high school sweethearts, but Lucy had broken Taylor's heart when she'd decided to stay in the city after college.

She'd been so young then. She'd wanted to see what the world had to offer, outside of Ivy Creek. It had been very awkward between them when she'd moved back, but gradually they'd become good friends. Just recently, they'd both admitted the spark of attraction had never faded, and so began dating exclusively again.

But she and Taylor were happy now, just the way they were. Why change that?

The bakery's bell jangled as a customer entered, and Lucy looked up from her musings.

It was Lenora Nelson, the matriarch of Nelson Farm. Lucy smiled to see her, and Aunt Tricia stepped forward to embrace her old friend.

Nelson Farm had been an Ivy Creek landmark for as far back as Lucy could remember. As a child, her father had always taken Lucy alone to go pick out their Christmas tree – a special outing for just the two of them. And as a family, they'd always gotten their fall apple cider and Halloween pumpkins there, too.

"Lenora!" Aunt Tricia stepped back and smiled fondly at the other woman. "How are you, dear?"

"Hi, Mrs. Nelson," Lucy said, offering a warm smile. "We were just talking about coming out to the farm for our tree."

She couldn't help but notice the older woman's expression seemed strained, despite the smile on her face. There were lines of weariness on her olive complexion that seemed new, and her dark hair seemed greyer than when Lucy had seen her, just two months before.

"Hello, my friends," Lenora greeted them with forced cheer. "They say we might get some snow." It was a transparent attempt at optimism, which fell flat.

Aunt Tricia wasn't fooled by her friend's light tone. "Lenora, what's happened?" She searched the other woman's dark eyes.

Lenora seemed to deflate, her shoulders sagging, and Lucy suggested, "Let's sit down."

She steered the woman to a corner table and Aunt Tricia settled across from her.

Lucy crossed the bakery to quickly pour a coffee for Lenora, black, as she knew the woman preferred it. She hurried back, pressing the cup into the woman's chilled hands, and pulled up a chair for herself.

Lenora stared down at the cup in her hands for a long moment, turning it round and round, before looking up into their worried faces.

"I'm afraid I have some bad news," she began, her eyes full of sorrow. She took a small sip of coffee to bolster herself before continuing, her voice grim.

"This will be our last Christmas. I'm out of options. I must sell Nelson Farm."

DEADLY BITES ON WINTER NIGHTS

AN IVY CREEK COZY MYSTERY

RUTH BAKER

ALSO BY RUTH BAKER

The Ivy Creek Cozy Mystery Series

Which Pie Goes with Murder? (Book 1)

Twinkle, Twinkle, Deadly Sprinkles (Book 2)

Waffles and Scuffles (Book 3)

Silent Night, Unholy Bites (Book 4)

Waffles and Scuffles (Book 5)

Cookie Dough and Bruised Egos (Book 6)

A Sticky Toffee Catastrophe (Book 7)

Dough Shall Not Murder (Book 8)

Deadly Bites on Winter Nights (Book 9)

NEWSLETTER SIGNUP

Want **FREE** COPIES OF FUTURE **CLEANTALES** BOOKS, FIRST NOTIFICATION OF NEW RELEASES, CONTESTS AND GIVEAWAYS?

GO TO THE LINK BELOW TO SIGN UP TO THE NEWSLETTER!

https://cleantales.com/newsletter/

Printed in Dunstable, United Kingdom